GUS LEE

CHINA BOY

A NOVEL

A SIGNET BOOK

SIGNET
Published by the Penguin Group
Penguin Books USA Inc., 375 Hudson Street,
New York, New York 10014, U.S.A.
Penguin Books Ltd, 27 Wrights Lane,
London W8 5TZ, England
Penguin Books Australia Ltd, Ringwood,
Victoria, Australia
Penguin Books Canada Ltd, 10 Alcorn Avenue,
Toronto, Ontario, Canada M4V 3B2
Penguin Books (N.Z.) Ltd, 182–190 Wairau Road,
Auckland 10, New Zealand

Penguin Books Ltd, Registered Offices:
Harmondsworth, Middlesex, England

Published by Signet, an imprint of New American Library, a division of Penguin Books USA Inc. Previously published in a Dutton edition.

First Signet Printing, September 1992
10 9 8 7 6 5 4 3 2 1

PUBLISHER'S NOTE
This is a work of fiction. Names, characters, places, and incidents either are the product of the author's imagination or are used fictitiously, and any resemblance to actual persons, living or dead, events, or locales is entirely coincidental.

To Diane, Jena, and Eric. The book began as a summer's tale to our seven- and five-year-old children, and resulted in our collaborative work. It is a moral lesson for myself—a father's reminder of the purpose of life, the need for both parents' love, and the everpresent opportunity for redemption.

ACKNOWLEDGMENTS

To Mah-mee, for love; to Father, for guidance; to my stepmother, for English; to my sisters, for caring.

To those who encouraged my work, with particular thanks to Lee Hause, Ying Lee Kelley, Mary Ming Zhu and Maralyn Elliott, to Susan Leigh and Alfred Wilks; to my peerless agent, Jane Dystel of Acton & Dystel and to Arnold Dolin, Vice President and Associate Publisher, and Gary Luke, Executive Editor; to Mrs. Marshall and Captain Piolonik, my high school and West Point English teachers; to H. Norman Schwarzkopf, whose faith in callow youth is still valued; to Bill Wood; and to HMR and MTH, who set the standard for excellence.

To the men and women staff and volunteers of the San Francisco Central YMCA, who ministered for low pay and long hours to the needs of youth: Karl R. Miller, Tony Gallo, Bruce Loong Punsalong, Bobby Lewis, Sally Craft, Dick Lee, Ken Cooper, Pete Joni, Don Stewart, Keith Gordon, Dave Friedland, George Wong, John Lehtinen, Leroy Johnson, Harry Lever, George McGregor, John Mindeman, Art Octavio, Buster Luciano Weeks, Dan Clement, Sherwood Snow, Dan Moses, Ralph and Lela Crockett, Lola and her cafe, and my other teachers and coaches of youth whose names could not be held as closely as the lessons they imparted. And to Toos, wherever you are.

And, to the Central YMCA Boys Department in Leavenworth—a place where all youth were of the same color, and every lad could be a hero. A place now so desperately needed, and now so sadly closed.

CHINA BOY'S FAMILY

TING CLAN

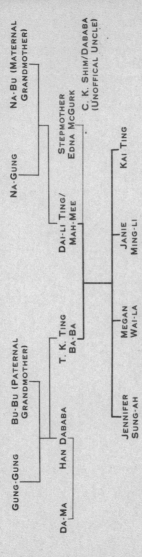

GUNG-GUNG

BU-BU (PATERNAL GRANDMOTHER)

DA-MA

HAN DABABA

T. K. TING / BA-BA

JENNIFER SUNG-AH

MEGAN WAI-LA

TSIATSIA (OLDER SISTERS)

MAR CLAN

NA-BU (MATERNAL GRANDMOTHER)

NA-GUNG

STEPMOTHER EDNA McGURK

C. K. SHIM/DABABA (UNOFFICAL UNCLE)

DAI-LI TING / MAH-MEE

JANIE MING-LI

KAI TING

HOUSEHOLD STAFFS

CHIEF OF TUTORS	HEAD HORSEMAN	JANIE'S AMAH	LEAD TUTOR	MAH-MEE'S AMAH	SEA COOK
LUKE HUNG-CHANG	MR. YIP	SWEET PLUM	TANG SU-LIN	ROUND PEARL	MR. WANG

1

CONCRETE CRUCIBLE

The sky collapsed like an old roof in an avalanche of rock and boulder, cracking me on the noggin and crushing me to the pavement. Through a fog of hot tears and slick blood I heard words that at once sounded distant and entirely too close. It was the Voice of Doom.

"China Boy," said Big Willie Mack in his deep and easy slum basso, "I be from Fist City. Gimme yo' lunch money, ratface."

"Agrfa," I moaned.

He was standing on my chest. I was not large to begin with; now I was flattening out.

"Hey, China Boy *shit*ferbrains. You got coins fo' me, or does I gotta teach you some *manners*?"

In my youth, I was, like all kids, mostly a lot of things waiting to develop. I thought I was destined for dog meat. Of the flat, kibbled variety.

In the days when hard times should have meant a spilled double-decker vanilla ice cream on absorbent asphalt, I contended with the fact that I was a wretched streetfighter.

"China," said my friend Toussaint. "You'se *gotta* be a streetfighta."

I thought a "streetfighta" was someone who busted up pavement for a living. I was right. I used my face to do it.

I had already developed an infantryman's foxhole devotion; I constantly sought cover from a host of opportunities to meet my Maker. I began during this stage to view every meal as my last, a juxtaposition of values that made the General Lew Wallace Eatery on McAllister my first true church. Its offerings of food, in a venue where fighting was unwelcome, made my attendance sincere.

The Eatery was a rude green stucco shack. On one side was a bar named the Double Olive that looked like a dark crushed hat and smelled like the reason Pine Sol was invented. On the other flank was an overlit barbershop with linoleum floors in the pattern of a huge checkerboard.

The Eatery's windows were blotched mica of milky greased cataract, its walls a miasma of fissured paint, crayoned graffiti, lipstick, blood, and ink. I always imagined that Rupert and Dozer, the Eatery's sweaty, corpulent cooks, were refugees from pirate ships. They had more tattoos than napkins, more greased forearms than tablecloths. They were surly, they were angry, they were bearded and they were brothers, bickering acidly over what customers had ordered, over the origin of complaints or the mishandling of precious change; enemies for life, and so angered by countless hoarded and well-remembered offenses experienced and returned that no one would consider even *arguing* inside the Eatery, lest the mere static of disagreement spark a killing frenzy by the angry cooks.

"Flies, please," I said to Rupert, who was the smaller, but louder, sibling.

"Fries! Crap! Boy, how long you *bin* in dis country? You bettah learn how ta talk, an' you bettah have some coin, and don be usin no oriental mo-jo on me.

Don job me outa *nothin*!'' His voice churned like a
meat grinder that had long been abused by its owner.

The Lew Wallace Eatery's proximity to dying winos
and artistic kids, its daunting distance from the Ritz,
its casualness in differentiating dirt from entree—all
were of no consequence to young folk who had tasted
its fries and salivated to worship them again. Inside,
food was ample, aromas were beguiling and my
scuffed and badly tied Buster Browns were drawn like
sailors to Sirens.

The Eatery was central to the nutrition of the Panhandle, but it failed to draw critics from the papers,
gourmets from other nations, or gourmands from the
suburbs. Passersby in search of phones, tourists seek-
ing refreshments, the disoriented hoping for directions
would study the Eatery's opaquely cracked window-
panes, the cranky bulk of its grill managers, and
steadfastly move on. The Eatery had not been featured
in the convention bureau's brochures. The Panhandle
was the butt end of the underbelly of the city, and was
lucky to have plumbing.

San Francisco is possessed with its own atmo-
sphere, proudly conscious of its untempered and eccentric internationalism. With grand self-recognition,
it calls itself "the City." It is foreign domesticity and
local grandeur. It is Paris, New York, Shanghai, Rome,
and Rio de Janeiro captured within a square peninsula,
seven by seven miles, framed by the vastness of the
Pacific Ocean and the interior half-moon of satellite
villages rolling on small hills with starlight vistas of
Drake's Bay.

The City's principal park is the Golden Gate, a better Disneyland for adults than anything Walt ever fash-
ioned. It has aquaria, planetaria, stadia, museums,
arboreta, windmills, sailing ships, make-out corners,
Eastern tea gardens, statues, ducks, swans, and buf-
falo. The park runs east directly from the Pacific Ocean
for nearly half the width of the City, traversing diverse

neighborhoods as blithely as a midnight train crosses state lines.

The Panhandle is where Golden Gate Park narrows to the width of a single block. It looks like the handle of a frying pan, and is almost in the dead center of the city. On this surface I came to boyhood, again and again, without success. I was a Panhandler. Panhandler boys did not beg. We fought.

A street kid with his hormones pumping, his anger up, and his fists tight would scout ambitiously in the hopes of administering a whipping to a lesser skilled chump. That was me. I was Chicken Little in Thumpville, the Madison Square Garden for tykes. It was a low-paying job with a high price in plasma. I had all the streetfighting competence of a worm on a hook.

Streetfighting was like menstruation for men—merely thinking about it did not make it happen; the imagined results were frightening; and the rationale for wanting to do it was less than clear.

Fighting was a metaphor. My struggle on the street was really an effort to fix identity, to survive as a member of a group and even succeed as a human being. The jam was that I felt that hurting people damaged my *yuing chi,* my balanced karma. I had to watch my long-term scorecard with the Big Ref in the permanently striped shirt. Panhandle kids described karma as, what go around, come around.

"Kai Ting," my Uncle Shim said to me, "you have excellent *yuing chi,* karma. You are the only living son in your father's line. This is very special, very grand!"

I *was* special. I was trying to become an accepted black male youth in the 1950s—a competitive, dangerous, and harshly won objective. This was all the more difficult because I was Chinese. I was ignorant of the culture, clumsy in the language, and blessed with a body that made Tinker Bell look ruthless. I was guileless and awkward in sports. I faced an uphill challenge with a downhill set of assets.

I was seven years old and simpler, shorter, and blinder than most. I enjoyed Chinese calligraphy, loved Shanghai food, and hated peanuts and my own spilled blood. It was all very simple, but the results were so complicated. God sat at a big table in *T'ien*, Heaven, and sorted people into their various incarnations. I was supposed to go to a remote mountain monastery in East Asia where I could read prayers and repeat chants until my mind and soul became instruments of the other world. I had a physique perfect for meditation, and ill-suited for an inner-city slum.

God sneezed, or St. Pete tickled Him, and my card was misdealt onto the cold concrete of the Panhandle, from whence all youth fled—often in supine postures with noses and toes pointed skyward.

Some who survived became cops, but more became crooks. We played dodgeball with alcohol, drugs, gambling, sharp knives, and crime. As children, we learned to worry about youth who held hidden razors in their hands and would cut you for the pleasure of seeing red. We avoided men who would beat boys as quickly as maggots took a dead dog in a closed and airless alleyway. The compulsion to develop physical maturity long in advance of emotional growth was irresistible. It caused all kids, the tough and the meek, the tall and the small, to march to the same drum of battle.

It was a drum tattoo that was foreign to the nature of my mother, but all too familiar to her life. This beat resonated with the strength of a jungle tom-tom in my father, but it ran counter to the very principles of his original culture and violated the essence of his ancient, classical education and the immutable humanistic standards of Chinese society.

Almost to a man, or boy, the children of the Panhandle became soldiers, until the Big Card Dealer issued a permanent recall, with the same result. Noses up.

As we struggled against the fates, Korea was claiming its last dead from the neighborhood, the 'hood, and Vietnam and every evil addiction society could conjure were on the way.

2

EARTH

My family arrived in San Francisco in 1944, in the middle of the most cataclysmic war the planet had ever suffered.

The family called the trip to America *Boh-la,* the Run, which is like thinking of the Hundred Years' War as a pillow fight. The Run was a wartime journey across the Asian landmass, from the Yellow Sea to Free China, to the Gangetic Plains of India, across the Pacific Ocean to America.

Even today, this journey would be a hardship. In 1943, it was a darkly dangerous, Kafka-like venture into the ugly opportunities of total war. A million extremely hostile enemy soldiers blocked the thousand miles of twisting river road from Shanghai to Chungking. From there, with a major assist from American aviation, my family continued to India, and from India, with the help of the U.S. Navy, to the United States. It is the type of exercise where one hopes for more than a cold beer at road's end. Since I was born in California, I missed the trip.

My family was not built for the road. My eldest sister, Jennifer Sung-ah, was fifteen. She was already tall, with long slender bones and a chiseled high-cheekboned face for which fashion models pray. She possessed unimpeachable status, for she was the First-born. She was resourceful, but was also a patriot, and experienced deep conflict in leaving China.

Megan Wai-la, my second *chiehchieh*, or older sister (*tsiatsia* in Mandarin), was twelve, and possessed of a charming and mirthful spirit. Megan Wai-la was as beautiful as the elegant Jennifer Sung-ah, but was poorly dressed. She possessed the strength of iron, for her pleasant disposition had been formed without the benefit of enduring care from our mother. Mother had, of course, wanted sons. A first daughter, with some good fortune, could be endured. But two daughters! This augured bad luck, and Mah-mee passed this ill fortune to the little baby girl who could be blamed for not being a son. Worn, secondhand clothes in a wealthy family were symbolic of a powerful devaluation.

Janie Ming-li was four, and enjoyed the dual status of being unbearably pretty as well as a near casualty of the diseases of China. She was at an age when crying was normal, but in a situation where a cry at the wrong time could draw a soldier's gunfire.

In 1943 my mother and sisters were alone in a world at war. All they had to fear were Japanese Imperial troops, brigands, typhus, *dufei:* bandits, rapists, thieves, deserters, and the unclean. My father was a Nationalist Chinese Army officer and joined the family in San Francisco after V-J Day.

"Earth, wind, water, fire, iron," said my mother. "This is what makes the world. I think I am earth. I crossed it, and became it, in the Run. I look at my fingernails, so clean, and still see the earth's dirt in them. Farmers' hands have soil embedded in the pores, so they are like the paddies. I can still feel the *Boh-la* in the little grooves in my fingers."

My mother's favorite belongings had been deposited into a crate that had been hauled across the world, defying the curiosity of interlopers and the efforts of thieves. It was a treasure trove of books, photos, clothing, and memorabilia.

Notice had come in the early morning of November 5, 1943: *"Kampetai* coming for the family of Major Ting Kuo-fan!'' the short Salt Tax prefect cried breathlessly. ''Tomorrow—dawn!''

The Kampetai, the intelligence arm of the Japanese Imperial Army, had identified Major T. K. Ting, Kuomintang Army, as an officer assigned to General Stilwell's Rangoon Headquarters. He was now known to be running in the hills of Hupeh province with renegade American soldiers, shooting Kwangtung Army infantrymen. He was being sought by their gestapo in retribution for his warlike acts. Our dogs would be killed if they barked. Sons would be bayoneted and hung from poles, the women shot.

Mother turned to Paternal Grandmother, her mother-in-law. ''Please. My respects to you, and my father. Please tell him I had no time to say good-bye. I must take my children from your home and seek another. Tell my husband!

''Tell him we will go upriver, to the Cheng clan in the Su Sung Tai. From there, Chungking. I would like, please, the old vegetable cart behind the tailor's outhouse. Please tell Yip Syensheng that the wheels should be oiled. We leave before dawn.''

In that one tear-streaming night my mother and sisters tore through their belongings, putting all they could into the crate. Mementos went in, sacrifices came out, but the loss was not material. They were leaving the people of their blood and the home and hearth of their ancestors, and their efforts were like waving good-bye to the world. They were leaving everything, from love itself to the best kitchen staff and cook in the maritime provinces.

''How can this be?'' my mother asked.

''Everything beneath Heaven is disturbed,'' whispered Da-Ma, her sister-in-law, who was higher in rank and therefore possessed the answers. Their children cried as they said good-bye to each other, fearing the eternal loss of irreplaceable friendship, dreading death and the loss of the clan's lineage.

When the cocky roosters called forth that morning, sitting atop empty dog kennels, my mother and her three daughters were already five hours upriver, stirring cool road dust with the chef's finest provisions and the house's best guard dog in the cart.

Jennifer, my eldest sister, looked forward to reaching Free China, and even America beyond, with the fierce determination common to the young in 1940s China. She did not want to leave the most exciting city in Asia, but her duty was to Mother.

Father had been born in 1906, six years after the foreign powers had seized Beijing in the Boxer Rebellion. Two years after his birth, the Empress Dowager Tz'u-hsi died, leaving P'u-yi, the infant Last Emperor on the throne of the Empire of China. P'u-yi and my father had been born in the same month of the same year, in the last dynasty in Chinese history. When my father was five, the Empire fell, and the warlords appeared. After the popular student democracy movement of 1919, my father's mother, who ran the Shanghai Salt Tax Companies Office in the name of her husband, foresaw a Western-influenced future. She promoted a younger man to be house interpreter and chief of tutors.

He was Luke Hung-chang. He was from Fukien province, was missionary-trained, and had bright, penetrating eyes. All my sisters remembered that. He spoke English, French, and German, was a ferocious reader, and represented the hope of a new China. He gave my sisters their Western names on their last night at home.

"Sung-ah, I give you the name Jennifer. It is very classy, very tremendously musical! A name Amadeus Mozart would have composed!" said Tutor Luke, smiling while tears glazed over his fiery eyes.

"Wai-la, close your eyes and listen. Listen to this

sound: Megan! Is that not dramatic, and beautiful! A name of love.

"Wai-la. It is a tremendously special name. And your honored mother appreciates the effect of name-changing. It will bring you her affection, and change your *yuing chi*. It is an excellent name change! I will think of it, and the sound of it, as you wear it in Free China!"

The tears now streamed down Tutor Luke's cheeks, the dark comma of his forelock continuing to fall into his glistening eyes. He knew their chances of reaching Chungking were not good. If they succeeded, he also knew that Major Ting wanted the family in America, a place he would never go. His duty was in China.

Chinese men are only allowed to shed tears when the cause is great. He was losing the girls of his dreams. My sisters remembered his passion that night, and how his tears and hair fell as relentlessly as his hopes. He knelt before his smallest student.

"*Syau* Ming-li. Little Ming-li. I name you Janie, the name of an empress queen of *Yinggwo,* England, the name of strong and good women of foreign literature. No one pushes around a Janie! So! Remember to keep your head tall, and straight. I expect you to remember me, and to keep this name. This would honor me, *Bohbohbei,* Little Precious.

"Say it," he whispered.

"Jen-nii," she said, sadly, reaching forward, touching his tears.

"Remember me, my beautiful students," he whispered.

In the vegetable cart that was their transport, Megan, drama in her name and cursed with being Second Daughter, looked back, fearing a future without the greater family's protection from an uncaring mother. She was twelve.

Jane, four years old and not to be pushed around by anyone, slept in our mother's arms.

Mr. Yip, the barrel-chested horsemaster with a Ger-

man self-loading Mauser in his belt, spat on the road
as they left the delta, heading for the danger of Japanese lines, the hope of sanctuary with our clan's allies,
the Chengs of the Su Sung Tai, and the heady promise
of Free China near Chungking.

My mother wept silently, not looking back to the
east. She turned to the north, to her father in Tsingtao.
She carried an unpaid debt of *shiao*, piety to parent,
in her breast, as heavy and as foreboding as the rock
of Sisyphus.

She also carried a wealth in diamonds, pearls, and
rubies in the lining of her clothing. Smaller gems had
been sewn into the jackets and pants of her daughters.
The thumbs and fingers of my mother's and sisters'
hands were numb with the accidental prickings of the
desperately rushed needles. The jewels were their
passports to safety in a world gone mad.

Mother feared that Father would never find them,
wherever the fates compelled them to stop. The world
was insane, and very big, the Yangtze longer than the
Great Wall itself.

I later asked Megan about their flight from China.

"Oh, Little Kai, it was frightful, and *horrid*. The
fear was—*hateful*. Mah-mee cut off all our hair,
smudged us with charcoal, bound our chests, dressed
us like peasant boys. We pretended to be stupid as we
hiked the Yangtze gorges so men would not look at
us."

"Why no want men look at you?" I asked.

"It took six months," said Jennifer from across the
hall. Megan licked her lips and shook her head, her
long hair shimmering in the light from the bright ceiling lamp in her room. She loved having as many lights
as possible illuminated. "We really were in terrible
danger," she said. "Mah-mee wore a butcher knife
on her forearm, tying it against her, like this," showing how it lay on the inside of her left arm, always
within reach. "She threw it at bandits once. We were
always frightened. Then we lived with the *Gungtse-*

tang, the Share Wealth Party, for over a month. Mother convinced them that we were peasants, and they accepted us.'' Megan peered into the distance.

''It was safer with them than to be on the road. But we left the Share Wealth village for the Nationalist capital in Chungking.''

The *Gungtsetang* were the Reds—the communist enemies of our father and General Chiang Kai-shek. I could not understand it. ''We saw so many people who were going to die.'' Her fingers rustled through the hair on my head. ''Father met us near Wuhan. He said to Mah-mee: 'I know you; you never give up,' and he gave us troops to escort us to Chungking, but they were killed. *Dufei*, bandits, and *tuchun,* warlord soldiers, attacked us. That's when Mah-mee threw the knife. Ayy,'' she concluded.

They had bounced and swayed in the old, unpainted cart, clutching the crate, listening to the hooves of the horse, ignoring the men on the river road, hearing the rippling tides of the Yangtze as it rushed to the sea, the dog barking anxiously at his new world.

''Quiet, dog,'' said Mr. Yip. He evaluated the road people. Refugees, spies, thieves, misplaced farmers, homeless, hopeless. He curled his eyebrows and his lips, promising death for their interference, placing the menace of his guardianship into their fantasies of finding wealth in the crate.

One of the best prizes of the redwood crate was a book written by Mother's tutor for her. Years later, she pulled it out to show me.

''See,'' she said, ''the character, Tang, my tutor. Oh, son. He was so wise, so deep. He always wanted to train a prodigy to become the tallest scholar in *Chingsu,* the Forest of Brush Pens, in the imperial capital. Instead, he got a girl who could never take the examinations. And I revere his memory because he also taught me about Mozart.''

My mother wept for him. As she related this family history to me, I twitched and rubbed her arm, which only made her cry louder. I asked her the key question about the escape story.

"Yip Syensheng and doggie kill bad guys?" I asked.

"Here is the character, Mar," she continued wetly, "my family, and Ahn Dai, my name then. The book explains the great philosophers K'ung-Fu-tzu, Lao-tzu, Meng-tzu from a female viewpoint." Later, I learned that K'ung-Fu-tzu was known in America as Confucius, which is as East Asian a name as DiMaggio.

"You change names, Mah-mee?" I asked. My mother's name was Dai-li.

"Oh, yes, My Only Son," she said, sniffling and giggling and pulling my ear. "We change names at our pleasure. For *foo chi*, good luck, or for better luck. Luck is everything. *Foo chi* is controlled by gods and spirits. Only clan names and family titles, like Mother and Oldest Daughter and Father and Uncle and Auntie and Firstborn's Tutor, are unchangeable, for these ranks were established by the gods themselves in the beginning of time.

"Your father has had many names. He was such a dashing, handsome rogue at Taoping Academy that he had a series of them, each from a different teacher. I changed my name only once. When the first Japanese sentry at Hangchow Gate outside Tungliu asked where we were taking my crate and pressed his long knife into Megan's face."

"You care for Megan?" I asked.

Mah-mee's face said: Wrong question.

"Father name, real name?" I tried.

"Of course it is. It is the last one he adopted at the academy. It came from his college roommate, from the powerful Cheng clan, of the Su Sung Tai up the Yangtze gorges from Shanghai. Father now works for the daughter of the Chengs."

"Where Yip Syensheng? Where doggie, Mah-mee?"

She shook her hand at me, since the horsemaster's fate remained unknown, but he was a powerful, smart,

and resourceful man. He was a survivor. He was probably shoeing a horse as we thought of him.

"What doggie name, Mah-mee?" I asked.

"Name? He was a dog. His name was Dog," she
said.

"Doggie live, Mah-mee?"

"The guard dog ran away in Free China. Tsa, tsa!
You are so much a boy, worrying about a dog! He
salivated constantly after the Run, and peed on everything in Chungking everytime the Japanese bombed
us."

As I grew older and came to see fighting as a way
of life, I wished that I had been born earlier, so I could
have participated in that grand odyssey. My father understood that sentiment, but it made my sisters think
me daft. In many ways, as a child, I prepared myself
for an epic test, an adventure that would measure my
worthiness to be the only son of the American exten-
sion of the Ting clan.

The Panhandle and the Haight, our mirror 'hood south
of the park, were standard-issue wartime blue-collar
districts where shipyard workers and longshoremen returned after back-busting, long-shift days at Hunters
Point and Fort Mason. The Handle and the Haight
were in the sunbelt, unique San Francisco districts
without fog, thunderstorms, or people of Chinese or
Caucasian descent.

When I arrived squalling—no doubt prescient about
my imminent fate—the streets were half black. By the
time I was in the second grade and in the center of the
frying pan, I was the only Asian, the only nonblack
and the only certified no-question-about-it nonfighter
in the district. Black families, tired of being ham-
mered by the weight of history and pressured by the
burden of being members of the wrongly hued tribe in
Georgia and Mississippi, were heading west armed
with hope and cheap gas.

That same hope brought my family trekking east-

ward on a U.S. Navy Liberty ship called the USS
George Randall, which my sisters, accustomed to great
wealth but sobered by war, regarded as the *Queen
Elizabeth*. My father's service as infantry liaison to the
China–Burma–India Theatre and Army Ground Forces
Commander, Joseph ''Vinegar Joe'' Stilwell, had
earned him a place in the general's heart and berths
for our family on an American airplane and a naval
vessel.

These families from Macon and Kiangsu met in the
Panhandle, a new and voguish rendezvous point for
those interested in building life from the rubble of sun-
dered cultures.

Our families arrived gasping, recoiling from shock,
happy to be alive but unsure about all else. There was
a feeling that something was owed them for this outrageous upset, for nothing that had been done during
the preceding years could have justified the insult of
war, the hidden costs of relocation, the tariffs of
change, the loss of life.

Blacks, for more than a hundred years, had been
fighting and bleeding under their nation's flag, hoping
for a share of the fruits of victory. They had all the
optimism of Dickens's Mr. Micawber, with none of
his chances.

During that same century, the Chinese were beset
by government corruption, foreign invasion, civil, religious, and ethnic wars, revolution, famine, drought,
flood, and excess population. They had suffered countless blights. The Taiping Rebellion, whose fourteen
years of steady siege coincided with the American
Civil War, had killed 60 million people. Foreign powers ruled China's coast and imported opium to pay for
exports. Legalized opium was laying waste the aris-
tocracy, splintering the social fabric, and threatening
even those too poor to purchase it.

China, of course, is not what a billion people call
their own country. It is *Chung Gwo*, the Middle Kingdom, the central state, the center of the universe, the

axis of the world, the home of the celestial heaven's chosen people. It is the home of the tamers of dragons, the sailors of the sea, the students of the moon. Until the eighteenth century, its armies and navies did their will, needing only whim to lash out with lance and sword to carve new boundaries and conquer new worlds.

The land of my heritage was like Big Willie Mack— its personality was that of an unfairly large bully. And karma had come calling, for all of us.

3

ELDERS

My mother was nearing forty, her rather perfect face concealing a third of those years.

Her five-feet-and-seven-inch frame was usually in dynamic motion, her delicately featured pale oval face, framed in thick black hair, was quick and precise in its expressiveness. Her eyes cast the mood for the house, and they lay above a molten and active personality that had the reflective calm of Vesuvius. Mother had endured family division, seen war and the destruction of her society. But the marks of loss were not in her delicately thoughtful face.

She was smart and probably more beautiful than wise, a woman who saw passion as life itself. She was like Sophia Loren or Anna Magnani, ignited by the surging and crackling impulses of life, inserted into a society of women sworn by Confucian edicts to apparent silence and conspiratorial whisperings.

My mother did things that most Chinese women would not imagine attempting in a state of final extremis. She refused obsequiousness, rejected submission, and exchanged restraint for spontaneity, stating the contents of her mind at the moment of the thought, however transient. She acted as if she were an enfranchised male.

This was the propensity of persons seized by *quah*, curious behavior, or of molten Italian actresses captured by drama. It was not the recommended mode of highborn Kiangsu gentrywomen. Worse, Mother used this unsanctioned license to speak her mind to criticize her own mother.

Her sister-in-law, my *da-ma*, the wife of my uncle the Firstborn Son, saw Mother as a revolutionary. That is akin to a Mother Superior suspecting a novitiate to be a Protestant. My aunt's cranium was analytical, mathematically driven, and poorly suited to coexist with Mother's passionate persona. Da-ma, it was said, believed that Mother was a repository for tortured spirits whose descendants never honored them in *ching ming*, filial worship, and were therefore never satisfied and would never know peace.

As Firstborn Son's Wife, Da-ma held higher rank, a position fortified by her bearing a son while my mother produced daughters. Da-ma punished Mother by ignoring her and encouraging her part of the household staff to do the same. These sisters-in-law lived on the same floor of the ancestral home in Shanghai, sharing space and tasks. Their enmity was poisonously patent, disturbing the geomancy of the house and causing the renowned head cook to tremble and overseason main platters. When Grandmother complained about this grievous failure in cuisine, she directed the head cook's assistant to make the sauces, and *he* overseasoned as well in order to protect his boss. Often, in China, it was difficult to fix problems.

Mother came from an aristocratic line that had more money than affection and more pride than skill. Mother's mother had scorned her work-loathing husband and denied his existence.

My mother was the firstborn, a station of unquestioned majesty and responsibility. She sided openly with her abandoned father against her mother, and did it seriously, maintaining the commitment in the face of popular disapproval. She persevered in her choice long after the death of Grandmother and the separation of an ocean from her father.

"Loyalty *is*," Mother said. "Loyalty *never* dies. Women who do not revere their husbands do not merit loyalty. Of course, I revere *my* husband, but love him more than I respect his authority."

Emphasizing her eccentricity, she dabbled with the spices of foreign languages and European music. To the horror of both her parents, she studied the Christian God and seemed genuinely affectionate about a poor prophet named Jesus Christ. Mother's portly maid, Round Pearl, accompanied her to the mission for English lessons. Round Pearl was very conservative and anti-Christian and feared the foreigners, but her presence did not impede Mother, or calm her parents. Mother's parents knew that Christ Syensheng had been hung with thieves for his opposition to traditional authority, and were only too aware that their sparkling daughter had married a soldier. They used to argue about which condition was worse, each blessed with the energy which only the self-righteous possess.

In contemporary terms, my mother came from a badly dysfunctional family.

My father was a descendant of warriors, whose line had atrophied in the three centuries of peace that China had won by war.

When militant Italian Jesuits arrived in China in the seventeenth century, they saw mounted shock troops of regimented and color-coordinated Banner warriors, bristling with razor-sharp weapons and quivers of iron-shafted arrows. The warriors rimmed the horizon with blood-red armor, pounding glinting tools of death against their chests and flashing cold ivory smiles as they anticipated the pleasures of homicide.

These men killed for the joy of blood and performed all functions, except the writing of sentimental sonnets, from their worn and battle-scarred saddles. They eventually suffered from an embarrassment of riches: they laughingly killed all their enemies and created their worst nightmare. A world at peace.

By the nineteenth century, Bannermen used saddles as drying racks for silk costumes and gourmet braising pots. They carried swords that had been blunted to avoid accidental cuts. Disputes were resolved by rash games of gambling and false threats rather than by combat.

When confronted by the modern armies of invading European imperialists bent on taking all the tea and silver in China, the descendants of the first armies to use field organization, maneuver, and gunpowder blinked dumbfounded, threw fine porcelain teacups in the air and ran hooting in a flapping of silks for their latrines, crying upon the Seat of Heaven to unleash the celestial furies.

That army, unimaginably, would worsen under the goading pressures of famine, overpopulation, and bribery. My father had all the attributes needed to be one of the great captains, but he was as out of place as a bishop in a liars' contest. It was my dad's sad fate to be a great officer in the lousiest military organization since the Children's Crusade.

My father's father, Gung-Gung, was a tremendous poet and artist who showed great fidelity to classic calligraphy, to high-throated, gilded-tongued *dongszi* singsong concubines, to his *kang,* the teak hardwood bed where he smoked opium, and to his fine, high-priced gum burners where the drug was softened for the pipe. He absorbed the poppy in a self-destructive fury. He pretended that he had no children. He was a product of wretched excess, when the very purpose of living had been lost through the oppression of wealth.

He was a matinee-handsome man who could have been an actor on the Mandarin stage. My paternal grandfather died the way he had lived: in disorder, with his sons facing the end of the world, their wives at war, the clan's wealth whisked to the winds of the poppy, his wife forgotten, his body turning on itself, the angered and exploited peasants at the gate unfurling red flags and asking for heads.

My mother believed in spirits, in bartering with capricious ghosts, in burning joss sticks to them in moments of reflection, in conversing coherently, and aloud, with her beloved father in Tsingtao while she was in a bathtub in San Francisco.

"The tub is perfect," she said. "I have come across the sea like the Ming admiral, Cheng Ho, to find this perfect tub. It is because of excellent deals I have made with the spirits of water and wind. The tub allows my feet to point to the west, toward Father, where the *feng shui*, geomantic forces, inspire calm and peace and allow the sun to sleep."

She once said at the dinner table—the center of life—that she wished I were a speedy forest and sea spirit who could deliver messages to my grandfather by air, wisping through space in the direction of her toes, toward the setting sun.

She trusted spirits in principle and distrusted people in general. She kissed the joss sticks to ensure that any carelessness in calling spirits to the fragrant paste during their manufacture would be repaired by her own attention to detail. She was superstitious, her respect for the unseen ranging from mild acknowledgment to hysterical drama.

A leading family belief—begun by rumor and concluded in reality—was that the only male child in Mother's first cousin's family in Ningshia had died horribly after eating peanuts. Whether it was anaphylactic shock from a unique allergy or asphyxiation from catching the peanuts in the throat, this is unknown.

But peanuts—eating peanuts—became the equivalent for me of spitting on an ancestor's grave.

I was eating a *chienkuo,* a peanut. *"TII-IINNGGG!!!"* Mother cried, making my entire body jerk in a massive, involuntary lurch.

The Chinese are wizards at homonyms; one word

has a hundred definitions. *Ma*, for example, means "mother," "horse," "locust," "frog," "thirty-six English inches," "hemp," "agate," "question mark," and "numb." Old and venerable societies need not bother with the invention of new words; the old ones will do, and can be reissued for new concepts if absolutely necessary. The Chinese, who outnumber the rest of the world in multiples, have only one hundred family names for all of them to share. Italians, I later learned, have a relatively small population and more family names than stars in the night sky.

Our family name means, among other things, "stop." So I wasn't sure if Mother was telling me to desist or was calling my name.

Mother picked me up as if I were a rolled blanket and whisked me to the bathroom, inserting her finger into my throat, causing me to deposit the contents of my stomach into the unsuspecting sink. Then she beat me on my back. Gagging and gasping, eyes wild with this insult to my digestive process, her hand pounding me, I heard her sob:

"Please, please, Only Son! *NO, NO PEANUTS!* It weakens your *shigong*, your vital spirit! Here! Take some *Chiing chun bao*, the liquids of life!" she cried, pulling the plain brown bottle from the medicine cabinet and pouring it into my mouth. *"No* peanuts! No no no no no! I did not wait my entire life to finally have a son, here, in this remote world, to have you die of *peanuts*!"

The liquids of life were extract of baleen whale pancreas, or supreme glorious squid tentacle essence, or somesuch, and always tasted worse than the malady it sought to cure. It advanced the use of shock to cure anything by scaring it out of your body, with immediate effect. It encouraged health, since fear of the remedy could exceed the harm of the ill.

"Mah-mee," asked Janie. "Why do *we* eat peanuts, but Kai cannot?"

"Kai is My Only Son," said Mother.

Even today, the name *Chiing chun bao* sends a shiver up my spine. But the whiff of a peanut-butter-and-jelly sandwich makes my stomach quail. Eat peanuts or suffer death-by-a-thousand-cuts? I would have to think about it.

My sister Janie Ming-li also enjoyed the benefits of deep-seated superstition. When Janie fell victim to infantile dysentery in China, Mother marshaled all the forces of the spirit world to keep her suffering child in health. She posted violent scripture all over the house, on every floor. She hung the sayings from the alternating peach trees and weeping willows on the street, and on the *wutung* oil, magnolia, and mandarin orange trees in the central courtyard. She burned money as sacrifices to needy gods and refused no petitioner her unique counsel. She advertised positive thoughts in a specific campaign to show the weak gods that she was not given to fear.

"My little baby girl is in *wonderful* health!" she declared with loud overconfidence to all who greeted her.

She offered to make peace with every woman with whom she had warred in the house.

"Honored Mother," she said to her mother-in-law. "I have wrongly criticized you for bathing in the front hall. This has been unforgivably dishonorable and disloyal. I appreciate your showing your daughters how beautiful your skin is, and compliment you on being the most beautiful lady in all of the Central Kingdom."

"Honored Elder Sister," she said to my da-ma. "How could I have questioned your wise judgment? Of course, I suffer from *quah*, for I hoard within me the despair of free-floating ancestors, abandoned by their unworthy clans! Please forgive me."

"Sung-ah," she said to my eldest sister, Jennifer. "I have confessed to my elders as they have wished. My yuing chi must now be indomitable and will save our little baby!"

"I have a sick baby," she told the best herbalist in the International Settlement. She described the symptoms.

"This is all for a girl, Lady?" replied the herbalist.

"You will treat this 'girl' as if she held your own life, Learned Doctor," she said.

"I will take your failure in her treatment personally," she added, using all her powerful nonverbals, silently focusing her fiery intent. The herbalist adjusted his wide, white medical headband. I know how he must have felt—as though the dragons of antiquity had come calling, the flames only hinting at the level of disaster promised. Mother had a way of making men touch their hats or make discreet lower-body movements to ensure they still possessed their manhood.

The herbalist provided thick paper packets of spotted-deer antler horn, Tian Shi Pian royal-red Korean ginseng root, griffin essence fluids, crushed foxglove, and Beijing royal gelatins for mixing into Janie's foods. Mother applied Zheng Gi Shui liniment and Dragon balm analgesic to her daughter's skin.

Unlike some, Mother did not cut her own flesh and add it to the pharmaceuticals. She understood the difference between form and substance, and knew that flesh-adding was all show with little curative value. The herbs had a pharmacological base; she was becoming a new-world scientist. Mother burned joss as she fed Janie the gentle, medicinalized rice gruels, bean pastes, and soy bean curds. She enclosed Janie's bed in heavy mosquito cloth to seal her from the spirits of sickness lurking within the family and required her other daughters and their servants to fast once a week to appease any jealous gods from striking the baby.

Friends were barred from the children's quarters in the house until Janie was three.

Episcopalian missionaries, to whom Mother was a mercurial darling, offered the magical elixir of Western culture to save the little girl. Mother used this as well. It was Cream of Wheat, from Passaic, New Jersey, and Mother always treated this particular cereal as if it were something found inside the Holy Grail by crafty archaeologists. Even Round Pearl liked this high medicine and she thought the *lao mao tze,* the Old Hairy Ones, the European foreigners, were evil incarnate.

"I'm not feeling well, Lady," Round Pearl would moan. "Please—one prescription of *lao mao tze* porridge medicine?"

"Here, toast," Mother would say to us at breakfast in America. "And," with brio, "Cream of Wheat!"

When Janie was old enough for hard-fiber foods, like inland broccoli, beef, chicken and long-bean, Mother softened the food by chewing it first. Janie was surprised when she discovered later that all food did not arrive in paste form.

Had Janie been born healthy, she ironically would have become the new Worthless Daughter, freeing Megan from that rank. Janie would have been the child with a living nonmother, cursed with being yet another in a line of honorless females and unborn sons. Yuing chi's, or karma's, downside is the utter ignorance of what one had done in the previous life to deserve the pain of the current rotation.

When it was unmistakably clear that Janie Ming-li would not only recover, but that she was probably the most robust child in two provinces, Mother revisited the herbalist.

"Doctor, I am in your debt. I gave you cash money for herbs; you gave me my daughter's young life. I owe you," she said, bowing. "Our clan would be honored by sharing any task or burden that falls into your road."

My mother's father, Na-Gung—the Outside, In-Law Grandfather—was a big, shambling broad-shouldered scholar with a large estate. He was generous with books, kindly to his daughters, quick to laughter, and slow to work. He appreciated the outrageous—a wonderful trait while traditional, Imperial China went to hell in a handbasket. In America, his lawn mower would have been hidden in the corner of the backyard in weeds and rust while he played checkers with children. His wife was not amused.

My mother, as was the custom, left the home of her father to join the household of my father. But her father had likewise left the home of their ancestors, taking his great library and Wang the fish cook to the northern port of Tsingtao, where the Germans were training dockworkers to become brewmasters. Here the crushing condemnation of an angry wife could be nullified mug by mug, fish by fish, book by book, chuckle by chuckle.

Tsingtao, from whence China's best beer would emerge with a Bavarian accent, is six hundred miles north of Shanghai, hard on the upper curve of massive Shantung peninsula on the Yellow Sea coast.

"Spirits," my mother said, "are perfect because they never die and never leave you. Women, My Only Son, have the great spirits. It is our gift."

Daughters, sisters, wives. In parts of society, a man and wife were merely a permutation of a boy and his dog. Women were expendable birthing organisms for the glory of the family. Mother resisted this status.

"Why must you always argue with me!" roared my father, shattering wine goblets on the other side of the city.

"Sweet honey," she said. "I am the one who left my dear father and brought our children to the Pretty Country. I did not argue about leaving that night. We left, and here we are. Your yuing chi is to hear my argument now, and to agree with me later."

She scrutinized naked male Rodin statues while thinking reproductive thoughts in an effort to make her fetus a son. Fearlessly, and in opposition to the embarrassed grumblings of her husband, she pinned pages from art books on the walls of their bedroom. The selected art was representative of the European masters, but the variations shared one trait: they all displayed the male organ. My sisters would enter our parents' bedroom and cover their eyes, bumping into the furniture with their shins.

Mother would hum her favorite Christian hymns while looking at the pictures, praying in her wonderfully eclectic way to God Almighty, Michelangelo, and the Yin, the Goddess of Fertility. She lit joss sticks, with some difficulty, and closed her eyes, visualizing male babies. She shelled peanuts, crushed them, and threw them away with the announcement, "For you, Watching Gods!" Most Chinese, like the gods, enjoy peanuts, and Mother was banking on the gods not knowing that she personally hated them. She attended Episcopalian churches and overdonated, murmuring, "For my Son, whom You will give me, thank You."

Hardly likely, of course, but here I am.

She did not hesitate to express herself fully to any person, be it the president of the Chinese bank where my father worked so arduously or a toddler, with equal force and elocution.

Men who made passes at her were not rude ruffians but agents of evil river spirits. She would shop at Old Petrini Market on Divisadero Street and wonder why men stared at her. In China, men of my parents' social grouping developed peripheral vision and would not gaze openly at women.

"River–Spirit–Men!" she cried after returning from Petrini's, throwing her tiny purse at her second undaughter with the flair of Sandy Koufax. "Why do they stare at me so? Why do they lick their lips like Gobi nomads at a well?" She put her hands on her hips, frowning at their misbehavior.

Even at the age of five I knew why. She was beautiful and wore tight, side-slit, high-collared, short-sleeved Mandarin dresses. She carried a parasol to keep the sun from her face.

She was an expert in nonverbal communication. Her

lips, eyes, nose—these were the instruments of discourse. Spoken words were not crucial because people should be able to divine the next move. For me, initially, it was like learning how to play patty-cake without a partner.

Unlike most of the known world, Mother did not like American cigarettes. But she enjoyed the eccentric radio commercial that featured a high voice yodeling, *"Call for Phi-ilip Mor-riss!"* and having Megan light them for her.

"Call for Phi-ilip Mor-riss!" she sang in a high voice, and Megan delivered a cigarette with a flaming match. Mother delicately puffed the expelled smoke, lips pursed as if she were kissing a newborn, and she would pose as if she were a European lady, gesturing with the cigarette. Mother could have delivered the Gettysburg Address in pantomime, using the motions she made with a lighted cigarette in her hand. When the smoke burned her eyes, she doused the cigarette with a thoroughness that was unnerving.

Mother knew that I had trouble seeing, so she would move her silently expressive face—the medium of discussion—close to me if she wanted her features to say something, so to speak.

Father, to introduce us to American culture, got the family hooked on the cinema. My sisters enjoyed the movies that featured Bette Davis or Barbara Stanwyck. Mother loved the escapism that films provided her, for she allowed her spirit to reach out to the women on the screen, urging them to success, to leave the undeserving men, to kill the bad ones, to protect the children. She felt she could influence the outcome of the screenplay by her concentrated thoughts as the story unfolded. Father went to absorb the values and the symbols of American culture, but never succeeded in making the diet a pure one of Westerns and war films.

"See here," he would say. "This man [John Wayne, Robert Mitchum, Victor Mature], strong like my army

friend, Na-men Schwtz'd.'' Father was fortunate in his
friends, but not in the friendliness of their names.

It was an American ritual in the fifties, when the
studios still produced a new movie every week, to go
to the movies as regularly as to church. Before Mother
realized my nearsightedness, she buried my head in
her bosom at moments of great drama, to protect me
from the frights of the screen. I had no idea what stimulated her actions. I thought people went to movies to
listen to them.

When something confused her, which happened as
regularly as the ticking of the magic clock, she giggled
brightly, delighting in the mysteries of the world. She
used to say that there was a small god inside the doorbell, and she called him the Chime God. We could
hear her laughing from anywhere in the apartment.
She, like Archimedes, had just experienced a close
encounter with a truth from the endless excitement of
the world of physics.

''Mr. Westinghouse and General Electric,'' she said,
''are *great* men! They have absolutely superior *shigong*!''

Mother loved ice from our kitchen freezer. Shanghai
summers were hot and humid, and the two middle
weeks in August were insufferable. Although San
Francisco summers are cool and foggy, she always kept
ice in bowls throughout the apartment in August, like
votive candles in a chapel, small perpetual ice floes to
ward away the sticky-handed gods of humidity that,
across the ocean, had robbed everyone of the pleasures
of sleep and dryness.

''It is *so* hot in Shanghai now!'' she intoned. ''It is
. . . is—hateful! Megan Wai-la! More ice! It melts!''

Father bought her a new Kelvinator refrigerator-freezer
on New Year's Day on the lunar calendar, February 4,
1950. I was five that year in Chinese counting, which
counts one year for the mother's hard work in pregnancy.
I was four years old by the American standard.

Mother stood in front of the freezer, standing on her

tiptoes, her hands clasped together, jumping, giggling, touching it.

"It's perfect! I'm so happy!" she cried. "I want a party!" While she happily cavorted, I crept up to the huge white smooth box and gingerly touched it. It did not bite, nor did it give me food. Mother's smile was huge, and I smiled at her, moved by her joy.

"Oh, no, My Only Son!" she hissed. "Don't smile so broadly for gifts! The Teeth God will want all your bright teeth, which you show so bravely! Remember— moderation in all things." I immediately clapped a hand over my mouth.

"Oh, Mah-mee," moaned Jennifer. "There is no such thing as the Teeth God! He would have taken your teeth and mine and Ba-Ba's and Megan's and Janie's teeth by now! And *you* are not moderate or Confucian in all your thoughts!"

"Tsa, tsa, daughter," she scolded. "How you argue! The Teeth God does not want women's teeth! And he is afraid of your father, who is a warrior! My Son, however—he is a musician and scares no one! And of course I am Confucian; I respect my father."

That night we recelebrated my Red Egg Ginger Party. "Red Egg Parties are held one month after birth," my father said. "To celebrate the male baby and his mother surviving birth. It allows recovery before the barbarity, the social invasion, of the family. And of friends. It allows time against disease, to know that the infant will live."

Red paper, reflecting good fortune, with bright, bold, gold calligraphy, was hung in the kitchen. The largest banner bore the name of her father, Na-Gung, and she prepared a special seat for him at the other end of the table from my father's chair.

Mother invited Uncle Shim, who brought groceries and helped make pigs' feet in vinegar, baked dumplings, and steamed cakes—special dishes that reflected the honor of the moment. Uncle Shim was a wonderfully elegant, silver-haired man with bright metal spectacles and a mind that seemed to contain all the wisdom of China. He had been a famed scholar by profession in the old days, in the old land, and had been nominated by my father to be my tutor in America. Uncle Shim used to call me *Hausheng*, his personalized and shortened way of saying Able Student. He had done great honor to my father by calling me Hausheng on the day of my birth, before I had evidenced the slightest potential for scholarship.

Jennifer and Megan made the special Mother's Chicken Soup. It brewed inside the brown earthenware soup vessel with the nipplelike lid handle emblazoned with the characters for double happiness. Dozens of eggs were boiled in bright red dye. The soup was medicinal for the mother's recovery; the shape of the bowl was suggestive of reality, and the eggs spoke for themselves. Father was a great cook and seemed to use every pot in San Francisco. He made long-length longevity noodles—not for their superstitious value, but for their taste.

He especially enjoyed this party because it was flouting tradition—it was four years after its customary time. He was a proud iconoclast, meeting the rigidity of the past with equal fervor.

"Why Na-Gung not here?" I asked, pointing at the empty chair.

"Oh, but he is here, Kai," said Mother.

I stared suspiciously at the empty table setting. Na-Gung was alive, so he could not be here as a spirit. Everyone said that I had trouble seeing. No one else seemed bothered by Grandfather's absence, or tardiness, or invisibility. His serving of food grew cold, and no ghostly, unseen chopsticks attacked it.

So we ate for hours, laughing and full of the joy of family. At first, I was afraid to smile, but Mother said that the Teeth God was dangerous when you smiled from greed, and that people laughing at food would never offend the touchiest of spirits.

Uncle Shim laid lavish praise on my parents for the

quality of the food, the effort in preparation. Then, after tidily wiping his mouth—which in no way impaired the perfect cleanliness of the napkin—he told jokes. Everyone laughed at his humor, although Janie and I were merely imitating the noises of others. Mother cackled, covering her mouth with one hand, in the Chinese way, and slapping her thigh with the other hand, in the American way. But Father's laughter boomed through the house, filling the air in the dining room. I blinked and grinned when I heard it. It was a huge, wonderful, spontaneous sound, suggestive of whales calling vigorously to each other across oceans. It was the sound of a dying race, the call of a species bound for extinction, laughing at the moon while karma closed against the throat. After these days, I was not to hear his laughter again.

After the jokes, Uncle Shim recited poetry in a lyrical, singsong voice full of great, shaking drama and octave-spanning cries, his face floridly contorted with the effort of creating a total spectrum of earthshaking emotion from the force of his recitation alone. He did not use his body. The Chinese language requires great intonation, and Uncle Shim was the cat's pajamas of tones. I thought his poetry was funnier than his jokes, but I often got things wrong in those days.

That year, when I was four, I asked permission to escape the suffocating confines of our darkened apartment. To the street. Into the air, to the magically beguiling sounds of other children.

Mother looked out the cracked window of our secretive second-story walk-up apartment. She lifted a blade of the graying venetian blinds as if it were made of fragile gossamer thread, as if she herself were under observation from an ominous, watching god.

Our apartment was a block from the Municipal Railway Car Barn, six blocks from the park, and ten thousand miles from Shanghai. She saw the teeming clutter of squalling children, the routine combat at the corner of Masonic and Golden Gate Avenue. Our neighborhood looked like a refugee camp, bursting its seams. It was. She shook her head.

Kai, said her face, you are not going outside. Bad river spirits there; I can feel them, in command of the street.

"All those children that fight out there hurt their karmas," she said. She ran her hands through her long and pretty hair and then looked thoughtfully at my chest. Karma. God kept score.

Westerners look up to God. My mother looked at the chest, the site of the true scoreboard, where all the ganglia and veins congregate, preparing to make final judgment on their host.

"There are fine musicians in America; you are to be one of them. I feel it," she said, nodding with a grand smile. It was infectious, and I grinned back at her. She hummed Mozart's *Jupiter* Symphony. Her face said: If you go outside, you will lose the music and become a ruffian and the sun will bake your skin and make you the same as the urchins on the street.

"*Wupo*, witches, outside," she whispered. "Devils." Accented by a shaking head, her hands, fingers pointing, gesturing, directing.

Wupo! Here! In the streets of America! I had thought they lived only in China. I trembled in fearful excitement.

Chinese believe in shaping children like clay. I still wanted to go outside, to see the witches, their evil little horns, wicked white hair, and red, gleaming rat eyes.

Don't make that face! she said with her eyes.

I stopped my face.

Her face was lovely, oval with large, deep-fired brilliant eyes, cheekbones chiseled softly from pale soapstone to hold haunting shadow and a mouth that seemed perfect in its fine linearity, its connectedness to the dimples that had been the common pride of her divided parents. A wonderful, joyous mouth that could laugh and grin and smile in a hundred expressions of precious, life-giving mirth.

She said the things that protect children from their fear of night, their anxieties about change, the terror of abandonment. I was so happy to be her son, her strength and beauty a shield against the glare of complicated and misunderstood days. She used to rub my ears with her fingertips, my cheek with the backs of her slender fingers.

"I love you so much, My Only Son," she whispered, clutching me to her as if she feared I would run away.

"I love you, Mah-mee," I managed, breathlessly.

She had the light, shade-cultivated complexion valued by Chinese aristocratic gentry. The portrait of her that was commissioned in Shanghai by the famous Japanese painter Nishio in 1932 shows a Madonna-like visage that stops the casual observer and begs reflection. I think it made happily married men review their vows.

She was proud of her rigorous classical literary education, but paradoxically cursed by a mind that could not grasp the simplest physical fundamentals of the Newtonian world: she would look in mirrors, bewildered by the image. She could never understand why the gardenia in her hair appeared on the left in the mirror and on the right in photographs. "Magic," she whispered.

I shared her confusion. Bread went into the toaster and disappeared. Burnt toast came out; so where was the bread?

She had come from a preindustrial society, where running water represented the New Age, and servants struggled red-faced with the crazed implements from Western forges, such as cars, irons, victrolas, and radios.

My father came from wealth but chose to fly airplanes, to jump out of them with parachutes made from silk, to march with armed and illiterate peasants in the yellowed *loess* muds of Chinese rivers, to accept Western military science, and to shoot guns at people for political reasons. He claimed Na-men as his best friend—a huge hairy foreigner whose clan name sounded like a summer mountain thunderstorm rolling down the Yangtze gorges.

Father loved the Americans. They were unspeakably competent with machines, were far friendlier than the Germans in the China Military Mission, and generously shared the best cigarettes in the world. They spoke easily in front of large groups—always a sign of deep inner strength. They chewed gum like tall, two-legged cows and laughed as easily as the wondrous, multivoiced, rubber-faced street storytellers in the International Settlement who spun gymnastic tales of lost lovers, lucky peasants, seasick sailors, and hardworking students, and rewarded the most appreciative members of the audience with the treasured white rind filament membranes of ripe oranges. Even better, the Pretty Countrymen, Americans, came from a country so young—less than two hundred years old—that they possessed no rock-bound traditions. In fact, they had no truly independent traditions at all.

Father had understood the present moment of China's history. He knew that the *Sheng-Yu,* the Sacred Edict of Master Confucius, could not provide the answer. He took to aviation lessons and the mechanical introduction to industrialized war as if born to the role. He was what the U.S. Army had prayed for—a tall, tough Chinese soldier who was fascinated with machines and could smile at death.

The American cadre clapped him on the back, shook his hand like village idiots and took his picture every five minutes.

My father's closest friend from those days was Major Henry Norman Schwarzhedd, an amiably capable Infantry officer of the American Regular Army. H. Norman's father had been a China missionary, and the entire family spoke several Chinese dialects. He could laugh at being a *lao mao tze*—an Old Hairy One—at the age of ten. He liked Chinese culture, Chinese agronomy, Chinese food. He could squat like the short-limbed, long-backed farmers of China's paddies and understood the basic elements of earth, water, air, iron, and fire. He knew the cycle of rice of southern China, the milling of wheat in the north, the occult kaleidoscope of the *Tao I Ching,* and the dominion of the weather gods over all life. He did not leave China until he was fifteen, his mind broad and grasping, his spirit kind and Christian, his tolerance unlimited, his tongue dexterous and international. Na-men could sit on a farmer's dirt floor and listen to stories of the Monkey Spirit for hours, laughing, nodding, commenting like an elder when he was only a child of eleven.

Na-men, as H. Norman was called, was fascinated by Father's strong grasp of Chinese history and had always asked for deeper discourse on history. Father and Na-men talked about K'ung-Fu-tzu, the moralist, and his *Analects,* and Sun-tzu, the Chinese theoretical master of battle and author of *The Art of War,* with a degree of animated sophistication that Father never had achieved during his earlier studies.

Father liked this big, beefy American who spoke Chinese in a strong and loud voice, and accepted the eccentricity of his family name. Na-men worked at his craft of military leadership as hard, as durably, as uncomplainingly, as Imperial Scholars preparing for their examinations. Na-men was a New-Age Man of China; he had no fear of steel machines or of the host of deities that populated the world. He knew that men struggle and that gods rule.

Most important, however, was the deep sense of honor, of integrity, that lived inside Na-men as it was supposed to in all men of moral Confucian rectitude. Na-men made sure all his men were paid and did not steal. He always ate last, after his men. He was the first to deny himself comfort and sleep. He did not use his position of rank for his own advantage. He treated

all noncommissioned officers and enlisted ranks as
men of ultimate worth, whether they were Chinese,
Senegalese, Indian, or *lao mao tze*.

The men in my father's family had not worked since
the discovery of fire, and it had been even longer since
his forebears had labored in the public interest.
"Serving the public" invoked in their minds an image
of busy waiters wincing under the blows of demanding
diners. Honor and high purpose drew my father with
irresistible attraction.

"Where did you go to school to learn this behavior?" Father asked.

Na-men said, "China. And West Point."

My father nodded. He had heard about West Point
at Taoping Military Academy. West Point had been
depicted in American movies.

"Hmmm," he said.

Father was trapped by human nature. After abysmal
treatment at the hands of his father, Major Ting had
been left vulnerable to the weaknesses of the human
spirit. He could not help but respond to respect, kind-
ness, and comradeship. Father fought alongside Americans. Na-men saved his life; my father saved his.

Father honored the United States, and its most
learned and splendid school of schools, the U.S. Military Academy, located at a place called West Point on
the Hudson River in the state of New York. Beyond
that, the Americans made movies, which, prior to the
Japanese occupation, had appeared within weeks of
Hollywood premieres in the Bund theaters of Shanghai. Movies were picture windows into a brighter,
newer world, where courage was honored and happy
endings were routine.

So Father's heart belonged to Lillian Gish, the Bar-
rymores, Thomas Jefferson, Joseph Stilwell, H. Norman Schwarzhedd, the Springfield '03, the T-2
parachute, the Vought O2U pursuit biplane, C-rations,
and the hot dog. His choices could not have frustrated
his own father more. Grandfather was deeply indiffer-

ent to the future and disdainful of the successes of his forgotten sons. Their failures or disappointments, however, merited his critical attention, which he would generously share with family, with his sons' friends, and with utter strangers. My father and his brother Han, it was rumored, had been beaten by their father when they were small children. This, of course, could not possibly have been true, but the very existence of the innuendo was evidence of a great moral ruin. I think I know why my father became a soldier, a professional fighter, and an iconoclast.

My mother was not impressed with Father's career choice.

"Ay-ya! *Soldiers* are killing our friends! And you *still* want to be a soldier?"

My father knew that the coming revolution would settle his class's long-term debt to the peasantry. The house of his father contained all the acquisitiveness and greed that promised the paroxysm of class war. The aristocrats would be the kindling for a roaring fire fueled by the fats of social exploitation.

Father wanted to live in America, where second sons could begin anew, washing the curses of five millennia from their blood and taking an oath to this new land that accepted everyone.

Mother accepted the decision to live in Indian country as gracefully as babies accept inoculations on their bottoms. She could not believe that the typhoon winds of change could alter our family. She cared little for wealth but believed that the powerful political connections of the Ting clan and her own wisdom about people would ultimately save them from destruction.

Mother had been a counselor to others in China. She had been called "Mother" by those unrelated to her. She was a social problem solver, a source of guidance to women and, through them, to men. She would have bargained with the victors, reasoning here, pressuring there, compromising in the middle, respecting balance, harmony, geomancy, truth.

"I am not a Nationalist, or a Red," she had said to my sisters. "I am, first and foremost, an honoring daughter. Second, I am learned in letters, as good as any man. And, of course, I am Chinese."

Mother and my elder sisters had lost everything—extended family, ancestral home, conventional roles, tradition, friends, teachers, wet nurses, cooks, wealth, servants, advisers, tailors, nation, customs, continuity, harmony, status. I do not think I have left anything out.

So being in America made no sense to her. Her inability to conform to the requirements of Chinese custom and family protocol, her helpless relegation to living without the extended family, and the continuous affront to her filial duty to tend her distant father, made her face flash with bolts of white-hot anger. Sparking with the unresolvable frustrations of the twentieth century, she threw dishes and tossed pots like the Yankees' starting pitching rotation.

A series of terrible explosions made me jump. I ran into the kitchen and the youngest of my three older sisters, Janie Ming-li, pushed me out.

"I want see!" I shouted.

"Don't go in! Mommy's angry and turned the room upside down!"

"Wow! Upside-down room! I want look!" I cried in Shanghai.

Mother had no fear of revolutionaries, of high office, or of broken dishware; she wanted to go home. Soon.

She loved electricity—ghost spirits in positive action. It was an affection shared by my sisters; electrical lights were icons of peacetime, of luxury, and of the ecstasy of nighttime reading. While interior decorators were becoming critical of the aestheticism of ceiling lights, Jennifer and Megan left them blazing in the glory of unsubtle illumination.

Reading one night under a lamp, Mother shrieked

in abject horror when the light bulb exploded, showering her with small glass shards.

"Angry ghost!" she cried, throwing her book high in the air, snapping the binding and exploding pages across the living room like schools of frightened white bats.

Jennifer rushed in to make sure Mother was all right. She unhooked the lamp. Using a small towel, she unscrewed the hot bulb and inserted a new one, replugged the lamp and turned it on. She then swept up the glass and reassembled the book, clearing the room of the tepid bowls of water that had once held ice.

Mother rushed to Jennifer and fiercely seized her arms the way a feral bird locks talons on food. She looked at her as if she had turned ox dung into diamonds or had explained the ancient mysteries of the kitchen toaster.

"Jennifer Sung-ah! *Promise me* that you will be an engineer!" she cried, peering intently into her Firstborn Daughter's eyes as she marveled at her ability to harness the forces of Heaven. "Ah Tiah always loved you so, and now it is clear that he was so correct!" Ah Tiah was Gung-Gung's formal name, and in his later years, my paternal grandfather had remained aloof from everyone in the clan except my sister Jennifer.

Mother drove a car the way an orangutan would operate a tank. Alarm clocks startled her with their surprising janglings, ice was overproduced, and our toast was always burned.

"Dark toast is considered quite elegant," she suggested.

"I have seen workers along the Yangtze Gong turn black in the sun. Not you. You are My Only Son, and not toast. Do some reading."

The neighborhood was changing before our eyes. Whites were moving out as blacks moved in. To my mother, being in Africa was no worse than being in America, for the greater family was in neither and the mother tongue was absent in both. But she knew that she did not understand the culture of the street, although she studied it through the blinds as later generations would watch soap operas. I did not know what culture meant.

"These people. They have been in the sun too long. War has been hard on them, too. Their clothes are old, like ours."

Mother walked me to school on the first day of first grade, my heart slugging with pounding anxiety. I wanted to go out, but I had been held out of kindergarten. I did not want to go to school. That lasted for *hours*. I wanted to see other children, not be with them.

"This is My Only Son," she said to the principal, an innocent named Mrs. Priscilla Wyatt. My mother recognized the type. Mrs. Wyatt was like a missionary, a brave and dedicated soul who ventured into the Third World with precious medicines and heavy, dog-eared, mildewed books.

Women could answer a moral calling by going to places like Hunan and the Panhandle. They could brave any responsibility for little or no pay, with only death or disappointment as the risks. Na-men Schwarzhedd's mother had been one of those brave souls. Mrs. Wyatt could not have become a school principal in Presidio Heights or Cow Hollow or the Sunset. Want rank and opportunity, Mrs. Wyatt? Go to the slums. Too rich for your blood? Go home and have children of your own.

"He has some trouble with English," said my mother. "I appreciate all you can do for him, in giving him very special help. We are not going to be here much longer," she added cryptically, her face saying, And do not ask why.

"He has a delicate and rare skin condition that worsens in sunlight. Please. Keep him inside the school building while the other children are outdoors.

Not knowing English, or having too much sun, could be very dangerous for him.''

I did not know whether to look at my mother or at my skin in surprise. I hoped it was not serious. My skin condition was this: poor little Chinese hothouse plant.

"My husband joins me in this wish, if that means anything to you. I would respect his wishes. You see, during the war, he killed people."

I do not know when Mrs. Wyatt uncrossed her eyes after that parent-teacher conference.

I was kept indoors until the age of seven, and as a result I knew nothing about children my age. Mere speaking and the use of my body in physical games and sports, as forms of social interaction, were unknown arts, as distant from my experience as the rings of Saturn.

I understood calligraphy, and I valued food. Of course, I valued food—the Chinese had mastered the creation of sauces when France was still Gaul. Small, children's chopsticks became my best friend when I was four.

I could, by placing my nose against the floor, and by being very patient, find the smallest button or lost item that evaded my family's search. I painted calligraphic characters with my eyes only inches from the soft graph paper, and learned from Uncle Shim the basics of Chinese chess, *shiang-chi*, with its bold, charging elephant, its austere general and his five *ping* soldiers. I could play American checkers by myself. I would laugh, for I never lost.

Uncle Shim had told me that I was to be *tsong lian*, an Inspector General of Imperial Viceroys, a scholar of historic proportions.

"The boy is perfect," said Uncle Shim. "He has a scholar's eyes already, built for reading and not for archery, and is only a toddler! He will be a great friend of books, unenticed by horses and the games of peasant boys! He will be safe from the physical world!"

I looked at the boys the way a Neanderthal would look at a dressing-room mirror in Macy's—not understanding the reflection, the resemblance, the connection, or the purpose.

Instead of possessing the native instincts of the hoped-for musical prodigy, I would prove to be nearly tone-deaf. This could have been occasioned by my later entry into the street, where my ears, and other things, were routinely boxed. For whatever reason, fists in the environment or genetic links missing in the DNA, Mozart's place in history was secure for another century.

Mother was a great believer in education. "My father," she said, "gave me Tang Syensheng, who was a Hanlin scholar, willing to retire from high office after the chest disease captured him. Tutors are for boys only, but Tutor Tang taught me for *eight* years before I had to share him with Younger Brother!" Her face was bright. "*Syensheng* means literally 'before born' and is an honorific. Age is *very* important, for it means the gods have smiled on your face every day of your life.

"I am happy that you like books. Comic books are good for you. What a cute little mouse! He will help you read music."

4

MOTHER

The Chinese are unabashedly social, for China's hard terrain and its labor-intensive rice, grain, and potato economy requires full cooperation for survival.

The Chinese lend new meaning to the concept of social interaction. Anyone can relate to other people, but traditional Chinese honor the dead. *Ching ming,* which means "shiny bright," is a ritual of paying homage to ancestors. Only the Chinese—who use the color white for funerals, speak to the dead, and leave elegantly spiced gourmet meals by cold gravestones—would use glittery adjectives to describe death.

Grave sites are swept, flowers placed, food offered, meals arranged at the headstones. The living explain new developments, emphasizing accomplishments, to the dead. Apologies are offered for imperfections in a Confucian world that expects flawless behavior. An unforgiving managerial continuum reaching from the father to the oldest remembered paternal relative sits in stony judgment.

Ching ming is probably the reason that so many Asians have succeeded in school, since honoring professors is simple compared to pleasing people who

have been dead for centuries and who have nothing to
do but judge your behavior according to the pickiest
standards known. It was why Mother's favorite and
most dramatic adjective was "perfect."

Mother could not practice ching ming properly because her ancestors were on the other side of the Pacific. No grave sites to sweep, no azaleas and oranges
to decorate a shrine, no direct communication with the
dead.

In 1951 we learned that Gung-Gung, my father's father, had died, his death confirmed by reliable sources
in Hong Kong.

Gung-Gung had been moved to a Reeducation Camp
near the outskirts of Chungking. It was a mild irony
that a patriarch of the old order had been sent to a
concentration camp near the former Nationalist capital, the place my sisters had called Free China. Grandfather's withdrawal from opium had given him two
extremely painful years of slow death. He had always
valued a simple, orderly, and fastidious life; it was
why he had maintained only one concubine at a time
rather than a large gaggle. This man of the old order,
who had more wealth than he could use, died in a dirt-
floored barracks without a pillow or a last smoke.

Mother erected a shrine. A dark teak table, white
pillows and tablecloth, oranges, lilies of the valley,
Gung-Gung's favorite mushroom pork dishes, glowing
joss sticks, all surrounding his framed photograph.
The photo depicted him in the days before he had discovered the poppy, and he looked glorious, like someone who would never kneel to age, communists, hard
work, or death. The acrid pungency of the incense
made the air in the room heavy and sulphurous.

As the Only Son, I followed Mother to the shrine. I
knelt once for my grandfather, once for his father, and
again for his father before him. I lost count and added
another, and no one complained.

"*Kow tao* for Grandmother?" No, said Mother's

face. Respect is for fathers, grandfathers, sons, bearers of the name.

The incense mixed with the smell of ling cod in soy sauce and sugar, of mushroom pork, and the scent of lilies and orange peel. I felt no loss, no sadness. Mother wept quietly for a few moments, as did Megan.

Mother then disassembled the shrine, setting aside Grandfather's special portions. She called Father, at the bank, and he returned home.

"Baba not like Gung-Gung?" I asked.

"Eat, eat, My Son!" said Mother, setting out all the dishes except those saved for Grandfather. She carefully extracted and then placed the valued fish's cheek on my plate. I smiled, for this meant that she loved me.

But this isolated ancestor's ritual was a unique event. Mother could not fully celebrate the Lunar New Year without the extended family. Why clean a house, pay debts, hang newly painted verses honoring the domestic deities, settle long-term disputes, and prepare feasts when the clan was not on the same continent? When one could not report to the watching dead?

We went through the motions, enough to depress my mother and sisters through the reminder of their separation from family, and enough to anger my father for the ritual's superstitious roots.

It was enough for me to become utterly confused about the relationship between the Kitchen God, who lived in Heaven and returned to the call of firecrackers, and General Electric, who operated the ice machine and only worked if money were sent to him in a white envelope with a magic stamp on it every month. As joss had to be lighted, the stamp had to be licked, and it tasted like an herbalist's mistake.

Santa Claus Syensheng lived in the North Pole, which was near Tsingtao, and returned if you brushed your teeth. But he never brought food, which was not only very strange, but rude. Instead, you were supposed to leave food for him, which should make his job very popular. If you were cursed with dirty teeth, Santa Claus would ignore the invitations to visit and leave you without toys, which had no bearing at all to teeth. I never understood why, if he were so popular, he was not allowed to use the door but had to enter the house through a cooking stack.

"What happen to Teeth God?" I asked, never receiving a satisfying answer.

Verses in bold, red characters painted on yellow banners were hung over our doors for good luck, while Janie wrote secret messages to Mr. Santa Claus and then burned them on the stove, like cash offerings to needy gods. How could Claus Syensheng read the message if it were burned? Only *wupo* could read smoke!

Great dishes were prepared for ching ming and for Christmas. But the best dishes were left to sit on a shrine for the dead in the first, and eaten until one was sick for the second. I went along with the motions, thankful that Uncle Shim, who loved to ask questions, left me alone on these issues.

The disparity between our home in America and the one known in China only bothered my mother while she was awake.

The utter isolation of our family from China was echoed by our partial estrangement from the Chinese community in San Francisco's Chinatown. We were of different tribes, and the difference was worst for my mother. Mother thought we were a microbial, disassociated satellite of the greater diaspora of Chinatown.

Chinatown was established against great odds by Kwangtung men, the resourceful and fearless railway builders and fishermen farmers from southern China. Their cultural center was Kwangchou, or Canton, and their three subdialects of *sam yep, say yep,* and *toisan* were incomprehensible to people from Shanghai.

Father spoke Cantonese because Taoping Academy, although in the north, had been strongly influenced by

Kwangtung men. Mother had not gone there and did not speak Cantonese well. She could not bargain for food or order a meal in Chinatown gracefully without using English, a tongue for which she now bore little affection.

Once, I wandered away from my sister Janie Mingli in Chinatown. Being Chinese, I entered the first restaurant I saw. I wanted a barbecued pork dumpling, a universally recognized dish. I was five. It was the Kuo Wah on Grant Avenue.

"Muhr-deh, ching," I said politely, my feet together, my head slightly inclined. Pork dumpling, please. I said it in Songhai, the language of the known world.

The hostess looked at me and said something that sounded like *"Neh ghong WAH!"* The first word rose with unlimited aspiration, the second fell precipitously without hope, the third seemed strangely complaining. She spoke in an angry volume that shrank my male unit and climbed tonal scales like a steam-driven xylophone. That was Cantonese.

I repeated myself. She repeated herself, louder.

She put her hands on her hips, like Mother, and I smiled. "Ay-yaa!" she said, shaking her head, beckoning to me. I followed her through a maze of tables, through a corridor and a door. The smells were heavenly when she stopped and spread her arms. I squinted and searched, my head six inches ahead of my body. I smelled and saw the basketful of *muhr-deh*. I pointed. Ahh, she said, smiling.

"Char siu bao," she said clearly, nodding.

I frowned and shook my head. That was not char-see-you-bow, or whatever. Those were pork dumplings. *"Muhr-deh,"* I said as clearly as I could, making the hostess laugh. She shouted at the cooks in the wild, exciting, undulating music of her dialect.

"Ay-yaa!" hissed Janie, breathless with her search of Grant Avenue, Stockton, and Kearney from Clay to Pacific streets. "I'll *muhr-deh* you!"

Murder was not an unknown theme in the family, because Mother had a driver's license. She refused to pay parking attendants because she felt the demands of driving horrifying automobiles were sufficient offense. After all, if she did not really drive, why should she have to pay once she stopped?

Automobiles. *Chi tz,* gas vehicles. In her hands, carts from Hell.

When the depressing un-Shanghai-ness of San Francisco and the isolation from her social niche overwhelmed Mother, she would weep while collecting us from school.

Throwing Janie Ming-li and me in the old Ford, she drove like a suicide candidate to the Pacific Ocean, releasing the straining parking brake at the halfway point when the hot scent of smoking metal reminded her to do something.

Every ten minutes or so she would hear the tortured scream of the transmission and randomly change gears. We would bob back and forth like horizontally thrown yo-yos. Her gear shifts sounded like twenty cooks pushing trays of silverware into an industrial-strength garbage disposal.

She drove with the relentlessness of a Mongol horsewoman, spectacularly indifferent to the vagaries of traffic or the subtleties of traffic signs. Even the great Jim Brown used to change directions occasionally. I think she regarded driving as something to be endured with a minimum exposure of time and space, dashing like a live duck through an arcade shooting gallery.

We looked out the windows goggle-eyed in anticipation of fiery death. Cars honked, brakes screeched, and drivers cursed, shaking fists and pointing digits. We knew how they felt.

She jerked to a wild halt on the Great Highway, bouncing us off the dashboard and flinging open her door, removing her shoes and dashing across the busy street. Janie turned off the engine and closed the doors. Mother flew past the undertow warning signs, down the graffiti-splashed concrete steps, across the thick sand to the wet beach and the surf of the Pacific Ocean, startling fishermen, jellyfish, and beachcombers.

My mother was the only woman I had ever seen who ran without Evil, the local bulldog, or a man with criminal intent in murderous pursuit. I ran with her, consumed as small children are in the passions of their mothers. She sighed as her feet found the wet sand, allowing her to accelerate while I still fought the deep, slowing mush of the dry dunes.

When I turned five the muscles in my legs learned to cooperate with the rest of me, and I could speed past her, hitting the flat wet plains of the forward beach first. Of course, she was running more slowly then, and I did not know it.

She was uncanny in her parking. There were perpendicular and diagonal spaces.

"Parking!" she cried. If we were parked straight, I knew we were in the diagonal spaces, and vice versa.

"Ma'am," said a motor police officer during one of our spontaneous appearances at the ocean. "You can't park like that."

Mother had returned from the sea, a Chinese Venus on a shell—a Ford—tears providing a liquid sheen to her cheeks. This was a woman who lied to school principals, pinned bronzed male genitalia to her bedroom wall, had a son who was going to surpass Mozart, and had produced a daughter who could harness St. Elmo's fires. She had crossed a world contorted by war, had traversed the gorges of the Yangtze, pitched hatchets, and bartered for her daughters using diamonds and rust. She did not need admonitions about *parking*.

"I am sorry, sir," she said in a voice that Marilyn Monroe was using that year, batting eyelashes that would have shamed Elizabeth Taylor. Gazing at him, drenching him in nonverbals, appealing to his basest instincts.

"Oh, please. Did I do something . . . *wrong*?"

The officer looked at her, and looked at Janie, smiling. He looked at me. He looked at her again, liking her too much.

"Ahemm," he said, tugging down his helmet visor, retreating, his motorcycle going *BrinDinDinDao*! in amplified exuberance as he roared off down the Great Highway, fleeing to safety.

Mother would sit behind the wheel of the idling Ford, shivering with her wetness, gazing at the Pacific like a fisherman with a hull-punctured boat. Her father was across the horizon.

She had put her bare, graceful feet in the frigid sea and expended two books of matches before wild fortune caused a match to accidentally ignite the joss stick. Sputtering in the cold sea wind, its sweetly acrid paste afire, it sparked to the spirits of the sea while she talked to Na-Gung, her father. The wet wind blew out the flame, allowing it to smolder and smoke, releasing incense.

Between my wildly unrestrained, unchained, free-from-the-apartment, seagull-chasing sprints up and down the beach, I caught parts of her conversations— her hopes that Wang the fish cook would bring a two-man pot of sea water with swimming yellow fish to Grandfather's home in exile in distant Tsingtao.

Grandfather would apparently cool his heels in the water on the hot and humid days of a Yellow Sea summer, letting the fish tickle his feet.

"I hope it is hot on the Tsingtao Bund today!" she cried into the crashing surf, the joss stick hissing.

"Then the water that touches my feet is the same that touches yours, and you can know how I miss you, and revere you, and respect your learning!" Mother had to speak aloud to her father across the sea, because he could not read her facial expressions from afar.

"Do you think of me? Do you forgive me for leaving you?

"I am so sorry, Father!" she cried into the cloaking

roar of the waves, the mist of the sea kissing the tears welling from her eyes.

"Mother abandoned you! I promised I would never do the same! And I am now in another world! Oh, my Christian Lord.

"Do you know?" she asked the wind as it carried her words to China. "The Americans made the black people their slaves. They took them from their homes in Africa. I think the war has done the same to me."

I assumed that our family home in Shanghai was like the Mark Hopkins Hotel on Nob Hill. It housed, at high season, forty-five people. It *fed* forty-five souls three times a day, every day, including Sundays, holidays, and Leap Years.

"Mommy. Can I run in Songhai home? Like at beach?"

"Of course! There is a high, upper gallery that encircles the inner courtyard of the main house. You can run around the gallery and pick the mandarin oranges all you like, just as your father did when he was a boy.

"I will also take you by train to Tsingtao, to pay homage to Na-Gung, who will be so happy to see you. He will give you the additions to the ancestral tablet of sons for the *ssu tang,* the family shrine.

"He will ask you to recite the Sixteen Edicts, and play magic string-knot games. Oh, yes! Let's do that soon!" she cried, crushing my arms.

"I have discussed our future with our Only Son," she announced to my father.

Father had received a letter from Amethyst Jade Cheng, who had fled from Ho-t'ien, escaping from the Japanese and the communists. She had arrived in Hong Kong in 1946, the lining of her coats filled with American corporate bearer bonds. In 1951 she had founded the China Lights Bank in Hong Kong, and asked Father's assistance in opening a branch in America. Amethyst Jade's parents had died on the Yangtze River road that my family had traversed. They had been unable either to assist my mother and my sisters or to survive themselves.

The Tings had saved the Chengs from revolutionary slaughter during the Taiping Rebellion in 1854; in 1946, the surviving Cheng redeemed the American Tings from financial ruin. Amethyst Jade Cheng was a brilliant businessperson who spent half of each year in London with English bankers. Until her death she never understood that Father, without her, was destitute. She presumed that a man with Father's abilities—flying airplanes, fixing guns and cars, being admired by American generals—meant that he could not have possibly left China without a fortune in diamonds and gems.

"Ah, gallant Colonel!" she would say, curling an arm around his. "How is the Ting family fortune?"

Father would smile painfully. "We have no fortune, Lady."

"Ohhhh! Colonel! You are so tricky! You must come to London with me! We will take all the money in the British Empire together!"

Father was seated at the kitchen table, studying his set of twelve banking-procedure manuals. He had chosen between his true profession, soldiering, and his nation of choice, America. To maintain his uniform, he would have had to live in Taiwan. So he became a banker for an institution that required as much travel as he had experienced while soldiering.

Mother said, "We are prepared to return home, while *my* father is still alive, to perform our true filial duties, *whenever* you are ready."

My father began balding about this time.

Sometimes my youngest sister cried for her cousins, friends, and wet nurse, Sweet Plum, a personal house servant dedicated to each child until either died. But my sister had more diversions than our mother. She was very good in school and had no prejudices about language.

For my sisters, America was a great adventure in

learning, in adapting, and in forgetting. For my mother, it was limbo, and I was her company.

I loved bedtime, when my mother sat by my pillow, holding me in her lap to read books that she drew from the redwood crate.

She read about mounted warriors who fought pirates on the east coast of Africa during the twenty-five-thousand-man expeditions of Admiral Cheng Ho in the early fifteenth century, about Bannermen archers who walked a thousand miles, crossing the Great Wall from Manchuria. They could break rock and bring down eagles with their arrows. I liked the swordfighting lancers of Hunan, who laughed as they ate with huge chopsticks from the largest menu in the world. She read about Genghis Khan and his Golden Horde, who had swept across Russia and left almond-eyed people throughout Europe. I learned of the lush southern colonies of China, called Vietnam, where the native tribesmen had fought the armies of the Chinese emperors for over a thousand years, prevailing in the end against what was then the largest and best-equipped army in the history of the world. There were few references to women in these tales.

I would follow my mother's graceful finger as it glided up and down the characters, from right to left.

"Writing is *so* important," she said. "Many of us are in this country, *Mei-gwo,* but speak a different *hwa.* But all of us share the same writing, and it unifies the literates.

"When you write, you can communicate with any of our countrymen, from Macao to Tsingtao, from Foochow to Chungking. If you have a daughter, after having *many* sons, please allow her to have learning, as well. Maybe she will write about her paternal grandmother!"

I asked her to script the characters for: chicken *tsow mien,* oyster-sauce beef, *muhr-deh* and *kuo tieh,* potstickers (a soy-sauce and vinegar-dipped pork ravioli). I kept the paper in my back pocket, and pulled it out as though I were Billy the Kid drawing a six-gun in the Kuo Wah restaurant.

"Here," she said, "is your family name. Ting means 'human,' 'individual.' Look at how beautiful the character is—a straight, strong, two-stroke chop.

"Kai takes eight pen strokes. It means 'reform,' 'educate,' 'improve.' I will ask your Uncle Shim to teach you how to write your names, for his calligraphy is absolutely number one. Your father will be leaving for Singapore next week, and Uncle will stay with us, and you will learn the noble strokes of your noble name.

"Your name should have come from Gung-Gung, but he never met you, and I never received the high family honor of your birth—a living son—because you were born here, in Mei-gwo.

"So. Here you are, so humble and meek, because we could never report your arrival to the ancestors. Your name comes from me. It is a very smart name. Mrs. Constance Carlson, who taught me and my maid Episcopalian English, told me that Kai is a Chinese name that also sounds Western. It became the perfect name for you, here in this Episcopalian nation. Our chief of tutors, Luke Syensheng, gave Western names to my daughters even before we reached this foreign land.

"Someday, My Only Son, we will return to the Yangtze. You will be so learned, so well prepared, that your future as a musician will be beyond doubt. Your music can unify traditional and new China, and my father will weep for the joy of you."

Her eyes twinkled, saying, And my pride in you will know no bounds. She hugged me, and my heart flew into hers.

Her favorite book was *The Tales of Lu Hsun*, which had been printed manually by the communists. She acquired a copy during the Run, during their stay with the Reds, and how my father ever tolerated its presence in our house has evaded all family understanding.

Lu Hsun described common village life, which was well beneath the purpose of calligraphy's highborn intricacies. Written language was for philosophy and poetry and was itself a demanding art—matters having no connections with daily life.

"Storm in a Teacup," "The True Story of Ah Q," "The Flight to the Moon"—these were the concerns of Lu Hsun. He wrote of food, farming, animal husbandry, and village storytellers, of shaman priests and *wupo*, witches.

Mother liked the tale of Tzu Han-ren, a five-year-old peasant boy supported by his village to reach the Pen Forest and become an elevated *chuan yuan* scholar, selected through direct examination by the Emperor himself. When he turned nine, and received his customary, first true birthday celebration since the Red Egg Ginger Party, the village gave him enough cash to buy three books—*The Analects, The Water Margin,* and *The Dream of the Red Chamber.*

Janie and I had birthday celebrations every year, in which we could order our own dinner menus.

"Why Tzu Han-ren only have one birthday?" I asked.

"In Songhai, My Son, we celebrate every tenth birthday," she said.

"So why did he have his tenth birthday when he was only nine?" asked Janie.

"Oh, it is to outwit the clever Birth God, who expects the celebration in the tenth year, and would strike you down if you enjoyed your birthday too much. Moderation in all things," she said.

"I don't think the Birth God is so clever," whispered Janie. "Don't you think he would learn?"

My mother loved education and revered scholars and musicians. I liked soldiers and loved to run.

"Kai. Recite for me the story of the good student Tzu Han-ren while Jennifer brushes my hair."

"Mah-mee, how do you want your hair brushed—back or up?" asked Jennifer.

"Dear. Please. Brush my hair so it will look wind-swept, as if I were standing on the beach barefoot on a warm day, singing to my father, facing China, with typhoons coming to me from the Yellow Sea!"

I was six when our mother died of cancer. I think she regretted in her last days the separation from her father in Tsingtao and the greater extended family in Shang-hai more than the deprivation of a long life in America or the permanent separation from us. Her death had begun when she left China in a cheerless lonesome dawn, without a kiss from her parents or forgiveness from her father. She was never to see them, or China, again.

If only she had shown overtly her psychic bruises, sacrificing a beautiful and ephemeral face, admitting to the ache in her heart and the loss in her soul.

I did not mourn her. As with so many things, I was ignorant of the conditions that occasioned change. Things just happened. First, I was told she was visit-ing friends. When she returned she looked weak and unhealthily pale. She neither drove nor spoke to her father from the tub.

She was exercising denial. If she pretended all was well, the evil spirits could not find a purchase point to take her away before she could return to China and her filial duty.

"You sick, Mah-mee?" I asked.

"No!" she whispered, her face saying: Don't ask more.

She spoke, smiling and nodding. I paid her words no heed, focusing on her bright, shining eyes, looking for the message that said: I will never leave you again.

As she had never managed to say farewell to her father, I never said good-bye to her.

I was then sent to stay with another family for a month.

When I returned, I ran into the kitchen, dashing

from one set of female legs to another. Jennifer's legs, Megan's legs. Back to Jennifer's.

"Where Mah-mee?" I asked.

"So, did you enjoy your visit to the country?" asked Megan Wai-la.

"I no go country. I Chinatown. *Who* those people, Older Sister?"

Our mother's absence had caught me between languages. My Songhai was pitiful, my Mandarin worse. My English was fractured. My Cantonese was non-existent.

I wonder to this day about that family, and if my visit ended a friendship. I can remember nothing of them, but I have a vague feeling of having been well cared for. I never saw them again and yet I owe them a debt, a gratitude.

Jennifer Sung-ah, elegant, confident, and firstborn said, "Well, Chinatown is *almost* like being in the country."

"Kai, did you finish the book we sent with you? Here, have some noodles," said Megan Wai-la, crying.

"Where Youngest Sister? Why Wai-la cry?" I asked. No one in our family answered direct questions very well. Janie Ming-li, seven years my senior, had also been sent away without being told of Mother's death.

This was traditional, to protect the young children from the shock of a parent's death while the adults burned incense, offered oranges, served spectacular dinners, overpaid for stupendous caskets, and prayed for the continuity of the family. Death was an important event, and respect to ancestors was a requisite, regardless of the distances that women in bound feet would have to traverse, regardless of the separation of men from their fields.

The surviving spouse and adult children of the deceased prepared to enter the prescribed periods of mourning, which ranged from a year to twenty-seven months for offspring. But without our mother, and the other keepers of the culture in distant China, these rituals were abandoned and I had only the vaguest knowledge of them. At the age of six, I was clearly within the age of nondisclosure of my mother's passing. Janie was in fact old enough to know, but Jennifer and Megan could not agree on whether to tell her, and there were no elder women to advise them.

Years later, I ran into a friend walking down Kearney Street, leaning on a cane.

"Gideon Chen! You okay?"

"My mother died. This is my mourning cane," he said.

"Oh, no. I'm really sorry," I said, sad for him. "Say, what about the cane?"

"Oh, yeah. I keep forgetting that you grew up without culture. The cane, it's to help us in the pain of losing her."

But Janie deduced Mother's death quickly. With fierce willpower, she maintained the custom and did not tell me.

"Where Mah-mee staying—I do wrong?" I asked, my speech compressed, anxious.

"What shall I read you?" Janie asked in a tight voice, while Megan rustled the hair on my head. Megan had always treated me well, despite Mother treating her as a visiting IRS agent. Megan's birth had created a family with two daughters and no sons.

Megan would become the most renowned member of the family, the one dedicated absolutely to public service, to world peace, and to the health of nations. Like all my sisters, she was beautiful. Her special attribute was her ability to draw friends and allies for a lifetime, based on fleeting contact.

She saw war in its simplest context: a man holding a steel bayonet to a girl's slender throat, and she dedicated her life forces to creating alternatives to the blade. Megan matched our father's courage in battle with fierce, gutsy pacifism.

Jennifer Sung-ah was eighteen years older than I and

was emotionally, physically, and culturally the most mature. The turmoil of China, the war, the Run, and the sojourn in India had made her wise before she had seen sixteen years. By the time she arrived in San Francisco, she was facing a difficult decision: should she stay in America, tour Europe, or run for Mayor?

She was the unquestioned leader. While she flourished in America, her friends would wonder what world-shaking changes she might have wrought had she not been wrested from the homeland. I still think that she might now be the foreign minister or minister of culture, perhaps Chairperson of the Party, to the greater benefit of the world. It was a great reflection of her inner self that most people thought of her as smart first, and voguishingly stunning second. She kept her distance from me because she feared others would think me to be her offspring.

My sisters cranked thoughts like Univacs. After a lifetime of being tutored and learning the world's most perplexing language—Chinese, in three tongues—they picked up English, a smattering of French, and negotiated American public schools and college with ease.

My sisters had perfected the English taught them by Tutor Luke by spending most of 1944 in India, where they awaited passage to the States. They had loved their English instructors, who were Indian and English. Jennifer and Megan still speak English with the lilting music of the British Isles, making many suspect that they came from London, rather than the English Concession of Shanghai and the Crown Colony of India. It was also clear from their internecine teasing that they had broken men's hearts every time they left one continent for another.

They both looked like Nancy Kwan. When *Flower Drum Song* became a movie in the sixties, I said that Nancy Kwan resembled them.

"That's not a compliment, Kai," said Jennifer.

"Nancy Kwan played a mindless tart, utterly dependent upon men."

In the next year, Janie Ming-li became my functional mother. She was the household manager, arranging meals and tasks with a military precision unusual in an adolescent. It was like a shipwreck, where the resourceful child passenger becomes the first mate. Father traveled, as he had in the past, but Uncle Shim did not appear in his absence.

I loved my sister's care. But a sadness dwelled in her, and I worried about it constantly. I angered her with my continuous questioning about its origin, unaware that the same sentiment lay festering in my persona, as insidiously hidden as our mother's cancer.

Typical of children who have lost a parent, we suffered eating and sleep disorders. For a while, Janie overate, then fasted. I ate less, performing an unconscious, immature child's ching ming by offering my food to my lost and missing parent. We tossed fitfully at night, unable to capture the winds of the sleep gods, and occasionally fell dead asleep in the middle of the day. Janie made our meals, laundered our clothes, darned socks, struggled to teach me religion, and made straight A's in her spare time.

Our father enjoyed Janie's home maintenance but missed his wife profoundly. It had been an arranged marriage of money to brains, and they had always argued about who represented which. But both people possessed exceptional passion for life and for each other. Father always loved Mother for braving the world to bring herself and their children to America; Mother loved Father for merely cursing when she declared her utter emancipation from the tyranny of the ancient traditions of crushing male rule. Their union was powerful, and unique, and never to be replaced.

My father began to rage over small things. Stilwell, whose mind was exceptional, had been surprisingly profane. The GIs had taught Father how to swear in English, and he got better at it. In China, his commander would have excused him from the regiment for the mourning period—at least a year. Father would have invited the friends of his childhood, his family, and his regiment, to drink *tsin boi* and reminisce with hot tears about the wonder and the beauty of his wife, the mother of his children, while he wore hemp cloth, sandals, and strode with a cane, the community allowing him to be nuts for a while.

In America he had no childhood friends, and he showed no weaknesses to his colleagues in the China Lights Bank. He had little affection for his absent family in China, and his organization, the 186th Regimental Combat Team, of 11 Corps KMT, was gone forever, obliterated in the bitterest civil war and revolution history had known. The wonderful, active alliance with the U.S. Army in China was history. He was now an American. Gary Cooper or Na-men Schwarzhedd wouldn't cry, so neither would he.

I could. I was good at it. I thought someone was hiding my mother from me.

My sisters crafted letters to me, full of details of the busy harbor esplanade, the Bund of Tsingtao, the fat yellow fish from the Gulf of Po Hai, the austere greetings of my maternal grandfather, and the exotic foods of the White Russian restaurants of Shanghai and Harbin. They read them to me, tearfully.

They were signed, "I love you My Only Son, Mother."

I wondered why Father received no mail from her, and why Mother had not taken me to accompany her to meet Grandfather and his tickling fish, to let me run in the compound's upper gallery and pluck mandarin oranges from the long branches of its treasured shade trees. I wondered if she had found Yip Syensheng, and Dog.

"When we go China, see Mother, Father?" I asked.

This no doubt made my father feel that he needed to find a mother for me, one who was older than thirteen, to cleanse the house of the complications of family consideration.

He had come from a lineage in which men had neither participated in childrearing nor generated income for a span of five generations. Such were the grand advantages of wealth.

Father had refused his roots, recognizing in American soldiery the beauty of action, the seduction of decisiveness, the satisfaction of utter and honorable commitment of dedicating his life to the safety of others.

"It is no longer good enough to measure a man by what he knows," he said. "That is the old world, the old China, standard.

"Now what counts is this: what can a man *do*?

"All the knowledge of the teachings of the philosophers means *nothing* against an airplane with guns and a pilot who knows how to kill."

So Father moved the family to safety, from a corner of the world saturated in blood. He moved his wife and children to *Mei-gwo*, the Beautiful Nation, the Pretty Country, so ripe with promise, unsullied by rapacious foreign invasion, uncomplicated by a cultural heritage that was heavier than its people.

America was blessed with a West Point, filled with movie theaters, far removed from debilitating superstition and the enduring memory of his critical father. My father had found his home.

5

EDNA

Nine years after the Run and seven years after my birth in America, Revolution arrived. It came in the corporeal form of Edna Madalyn McGurk.

She smelled like roses. She was a college graduate in English literature from Smith, was primly handsome, and had missed her calling when the SS closed its ranks to all comers after the demise of Hitler.

Our father married her for my sake, although I thought he had generously exceeded my needs. I understood the part about having a mother, because by the time Stepmother Edna was sworn into office, a year had passed since I had seen mine. My mother's letters from China had shifted from the lackluster and the infrequent to the nonexistent. I began to fear that she would neither return nor call for me and Janie to join her, and was even more fearful of the cause of her break in correspondence.

My yuing chi, my karma, was bad. Not bad. Terrible. I had not scored well in God's book. I struggled to determine what I had done to make my mother stay away for a year, wanting to never do it again. It was so baffling, for I felt as if I had behaved correctly, trying to help Ming-li raise me.

"Good morning," Edna said, with a blinding smile, the echo of her clacking heels loud on the hardwood floor of our hallway. She looked like a movie star— tall, angular, and confident. She had a very attractive, bright-eyed face and light, sunny blond hair that fascinated me. It was like looking at a well-dressed light bulb. She looked remotely like a Western version of Mother.

"My, you're just adorable. So cute!" She was wearing a dark navy pillbox hat with a veil and matching wasp-waisted dress. She demonstrated her dexterity by managing to pinch my cheek while wearing elbow-length white gloves. It hurt a little.

"You may call me Stepmother Edna." I could pronounce none of it. She was luminously gorgeous, and I loved her.

Unlike us, Edna was a direct person, providing absolutely precise answers to cosmic inquiries. We learned to dislike her answers. I listened carefully to her because she was tall, had perfect diction, looked wonderful, and scared me down to my socks.

She was *nahgwangning*. Foreign country person. Tremendously exotic. I couldn't wait to see how she drove a car. Her face was slender, illuminated in the center by pale gray eyes and shimmering in its blond outline. Her face was rather immobile. She spoke with her tongue and lips, and not her face.

Edna McGurk came from an insular inner circle of elite Philadelphia society. She came to our house the way the Germans marched into Paris, certain of conquest and totally prepared to suppress resistance.

Six years before, she had shocked her family and class by marrying a destitute Berkeley law student. He was a solid fellow, a World War II vet who was on his way to a good life with her when he was drafted for the Korean War.

Chinese communist troops killed him on the banks

of the Imjin River in the winter offensive of 1950. He had died under the guns of Chu Teh's infantrymen of the People's Liberation Eighth Route Army, the same guys who had dropkicked my father's former regiments across the Formosa Strait the year before. The same guys, by their thoughtless acts, had managed to place Edna, angry and sad, into our immigrant home.

I do not know how Edna coped with her loss. As with so many military casualties, the ordeal began with reports that he was missing in action, followed by possible POW status, and concluding with final regrets. His remains were returned with military honors. I think part of Father's attractiveness to her was premised on his survival through the test of an extended war record.

Their meeting was an arabesque, orchestrated by a USO function at the Geary Theatre for veterans and widows. The prime attraction was Danny Kaye. The audience roared and punished its hands in endless applause. Amid this eruption of celebrational goodwill, manners became expendable, petting was rampant, and booze was in the air. "Thank you, thank you," Danny Kaye was saying, as Colonel Ting and Mrs. McGurk were jostled together at the lobby bar.

"Make mine Coke," they uttered simultaneously, laughing and admiring each other for their common demonstration of restraint. The recognition each saw in the other was instantaneous. The exotica of their contrasts, the attraction of shared height, the patent, irresistible marks of loss in their eyes, drew them elbow to elbow, gazing at each other. Edna was captivated by what she termed a cosmic sweetness. Heightened by the remembrance of war, softened by the light brush of comedy, strengthened by the common bond of need.

"My name is T.K. Ting," he said, passing her the soda.

"I am Edna McGurk," she replied, offering her

hand, searching for confirmation of the heady spark that had illuminated the smoke-filled lobby.

He learned that she was from the East Coast, loved Shakespeare and Gauguin, believed in a God that favored no particular faith, and had read all the books of Pearl Buck. And that she was the only member of her family to leave Pennsylvania and had long fantasized about flying in the open cockpit of an airplane, wearing goggles and a scarf. She confessed to becoming giddy with a few drinks, slipping curiously into an Irish brogue.

"I'm a widow, but not a merry one," she said.

"Fate can be cruel, but in America, it can change," replied Father.

She learned that he had been classically educated in China, had fought alongside the American army, had been a pilot, and was the only member of his family to leave China. That he thought she resembled the actress Lana Turner, and that his wife had died very recently.

Edna had loved her first husband, and was swept away by her second. She arrived in our home silently grieving for one while openly adoring Father. We mourned the absence of our mother. Both Father and Edna had lost their lives' true loves, and were doing the best they could manage. The children were to prove liabilities to their plans.

"I am going to be your mother," she announced, removing the hat while aligning the veil. "It's going to be wonderful."

Neither Father nor Edna were friends of indecision. The wedding was over and Edna had moved into the master bedroom. I never knew the impetus for their speed, but I think they were fleeing reason, preferring to throw the dice and go for broke rather than take another chance on a lonely tomorrow.

Father gained notice for marrying a beautiful foreigner, and had taken a major-league step toward cementing the American assimilation he so desperately sought. Edna proved that her first marriage to a commoner was no quirk; she picked her husbands premised on her own, very individual tastes.

Nor was Edna one to take open counsel of her fears. She joined our ragged little household with an abruptness that was unknown to it.

"I can't *stand* how *everyone* in this house speaks!" I thought she was referring to my sisters' English accents until I realized that "everyone" was me.

I also showed an early lack of communication proficiency.

"When *tsow mien?*" I asked, lacking only the empty bowl in my hands to complete the effect. Stepmother Edna looked so smart; she had to understand that I was requesting noodles, the food of the gods. Even the Italians had adopted it after Marco Polo brought the strands back through the Silk Route.

She studied me, like bird droppings on a Rolls-Royce.

"*What* is 'sow men'?"

"*Tsow-mien,*" I said, louder.

Her toe began tapping. I looked at it.

"I cannot understand that barbaric speech," she said. "Do not talk to me unless you are prepared to speak *English*. And don't look at me like that!" The toe stopped. Her fist balled.

I knew what that meant. But I was wrong; it meant much more than, yes, we have no noodles.

"Young man, you are now an American. You are very cute, but you cannot get by in this world by looking endearingly at people. You must give up your past habits and learn new ones.

"You also look quite sickly, and you make so many—faces," she said. "I will teach you English, and you *will* learn. This will save you from becoming a ditchdigger or a drayman. It should also improve your facial expressions."

Edna was placing the kitchen in order. Because Janie was not very tall, everything in the lower cabinet shelves had been organized in the year of our mother's absence. Everything above Janie's height was cluttered.

Edna seemed angry as she spoke, moving cups and dishes. She was standing on a chair, and her hair wafted across her face until she wrapped it up atop her head. Her nose was aquiline and sharp, like Uncle Shim's, although she was considerably prettier. She liked neither the kitchen's condition nor the effort involved in its reorganization. I knew she viewed me in the same light.

I marveled at her physical beauty, wanting her to like me, to read to me, to even hold me. I remembered, looking at her, that my mother used to kiss my nose in the morning, her cup of steaming white tea misting her face.

"Stepma kiss nose?" I asked, using my hands and face more than my speech.

"Pardon me?" she asked crisply.

"You need to go outside and fill your hollow chest with fresh air. Truly *normal* seven-year-olds play outside. Now, shoo! If I want you, I'll whistle, like this," and she made the sound of a London constable car siren.

I did not know that then. I thought it sounded like Mr. Carter's whistle. Mother and I had seen him use the whistle to call Evil, his bulldog, after it had started to chew on short human legs. The whistle was shrill and had to be louder than a child's mortal cries.

I stood there, ear wax melting, ear drums erupting, and eyes popping.

I tried to tell her that I had this special skin condition, which worsened in sunlight. But only Chinese Mulligan Stew, wild with crisscrossed *r*'s and *l*'s, with deep-forested diphthongs and evergreened interdentals, came out of my struggling mouth.

The street waited for me the way a mako shark awaits limbs hanging from inner tubes.

The street was filled with my peers. War babies, the

Baby Boomers. There were more of us in the two-through-seven age group than in all the others combined. We were a huge club. My membership card had not arrived in the mail.

Some of the street kids had seen me before. I would zoom down Central past the huge, redbrick Municipal Railway Car Barn to McAllister and pull a screaming left. I would hoof it with high-pumping knee action to Fremont Elementary on Broderick like Pacific storm winds howling off Twin Peaks. I left for school before most kids were up, honing those high-achievement skills early.

During recess, I hovered near teachers, the natural allies of pint-sized Asian students. Away from the protective radius of the faculty, kids were being beaten dumb by other kids. These children are cashing in their futures, I thought. During class, I pretended I was not there, a small ghost my mother would have understood, a spirit with whom she might commune.

The slum schoolteachers of the fifties were as resourceful as atomic-bomb survivors, a status for which they had been trained. These were the days of ducking and cowering under our desks to survive a direct hit from an atomic bomb.

Mr. Isington was from England. He had a refined accent like Jennifer's and Megan's. An expatriate, he had been in the Canadian Army, landing on Normandy and staying in the war until the end. He was short, squat, had a feral sense of survival, and smelled of baby powder. Kids backed off when he began tugging at the end of his nose, as if he were extending the muzzle of a gun.

He was a no-nonsense chap. Mr. Isington operated like the Claudian emperors, with his own Praetorian Guard. He formed a band of monolithic sixth-graders, and enforced classroom discipline with flying-wing tactics.

He called them the Bomb Squad—the first youth gang created under color of governmental fiat since the alley mobs of Scilla. They were guided by the axiom "Might makes right" and manned by thugs who accepted higher authority. They were probably Young Republicans.

Mr. Isington later told me that Big Willie Mack, my enemy on the streets, had asked if he could join the Bombers and had been refused. That, in retrospect, was a big mistake. Cop or crook, the turn of a screw. What if Big Willie had become a rescuing Bomber, and not a thunderous bully? What if someone in Vienna had taken young Adolf Hitler's efforts at architecture seriously?

Fighting in class was normal. When it became a riot, teachers cried "Help!" through the door transoms into the hallway. The hall monitors passed the word like the Pony Express.

"By Jove, lads," said Mr. Isington on the scratchy, static-filled squawk box, "we have an incident in Room 20, Mrs. Halloran's. Be so good as to bustle down there, if you would. Hall monitors, keep to your stations. That's good, young gentlemen." And the Bomb Squaders would leave their sixth-grade seats and trash the offenders.

Mrs. Halloran showed her teeth in a sickened smile while organized battery was committed in the name of order, suspending for the moment our lesson about the wild beasts of the Fleischacker Zoo.

I came home from school as I had arrived: fast, my feet barely touching the pavement. At the age of seven, without outdoor play but with the history of the dunes, I had learned to pump my legs and arms high like a hurdler sprinting for the tape. I had learned to run as baby starlings learn to eat predigested pabulum, or as Janie had eaten prechewed broccoli from our mother. Because it was necessary.

Other kids were too happy at the 3:10 bell to worry about the little Chinese squirt beating feet for his life. I would enter the sanctuary of our apartment breathing hard and filled with the relief of escape.

American culture was a mystery, the evolving black subculture of the Panhandle was an enigma, and both overlapped across my struggling mind like a galloping herd of octopuses; I had trouble distinguishing the origin of the tentacles. But foreign or not, I knew I did not want to get beaten up.

Some of the preschool kids on the block did not think I was human. They had not seen my dawn runs to the school. So when Edna evicted me, they touched my hands and face, wondering where all the color had gone. And what had happened to my hair?

"Man," said one of them. "He so ugly. Doctah pull him out, doctah slap his momma 'steada him!"

"Don't say *nothin* 'bout no mommas!" said someone else.

I wanted to hear *more* about mommas. Anyone's momma.

Some of the kids were old enough to know that I belonged to a group of people who had attacked Pearl Harbor and cooked terribly stinky food in funny restaurants. I would later learn to my great relief that my mother and father did not attack Pearl Harbor.

"Jap," said one.

"Chink!" said another. "He a Chink, not a Jap!"

My heart had gone from beating two hundred times a minute to All Engines Stop. My psychic apparatus told me that Jap or Chink, I was in deep trouble.

I thought Pearl Habba was an unlucky victim of the Fremont schoolyard. That Pearl was probably a kid who couldn't run like the wind. A kid who got thrown out of sanctuary to become dog meat. Food for Evil, the dog.

If you've got the blood, we've got the fists. It's Alpo time.

The two kids who could not agree on the ethnicity of my origin pushed each other for a few seconds. A circle formed. Then they beat each other up. This was the pattern of the schoolyard. I ran for my door. It was locked. I knew how Hansel and Gretel felt in the scary woods. I rang the doorbell as sincerely as I could, and Edna appeared, like Pinocchio's fairy godmother. We all looked at her. Even I stared as if I had not seen her before. She was blond. She did not seem to like Chinese food, made unusual noises, and was proudly violent. She was *wupo*! Ay-ya! They *were* in America! And they opened doors!

"T'ank you!" I gushed.

"Now, I didn't whistle for you. You just went out." She was staring directly at my terrified face, ignoring the mob. "Go make friends." Slam, click.

Scared but ignorant, I descended the six stone steps to the street. The fight had stopped when Edna had appeared, and the kids were a bit dazed with the appearance of a blond Anglo-patrician on their block.

"Wow!" said a huge kid, who had to be thirty years old. "Who dat lady?"

"Stepmama Edna," I said, in my eccentric accent, and those who heard me laughed. Those who had not heard also laughed. I thought laughter was good. Wrong again.

I was not comfortable talking to kids, particularly boys, and I avoided the older ones like the plague. Now they were on me like raw egg on hair.

The group of children smelled my fear and anxiety. They looked like a homogeneous mass of clothes, heads, and arms. They closed in tighter.

I tried communication. Take me to your leader.

"*Yau pungyoh,*" I squeaked. I want to be friends.

"*Yow?* Yow *what*!?" The laughter was deafening. These kids and I were more culturally attuned than we knew. Chinese *hwa,* language, and the black patois of the Panhandle depended on inflection and musical tone and were indifferent to conjugation. We came from societies that honored families, war, percussion, and elders. These similarities, however, were not presently evident.

"Who she be, you ratfacedshitferbrains," said the mammoth kid, towering above the mob. His name was

Willis "Willie" Mack. Big Willie, "big" as a dirigible hangar. Mack, as in truck. Willis, as in nemesis.

I stared blankly, his meaning lost. He said it again, louder.

I yelled as something incredibly hurtful hit my chest and I went backward on the step, hitting the back of my head. Shocked and feeling pain, I began to cry. Something else hit me and now, convinced that death was calling, I wailed with all my might. I was calling to Janie, Megan, and Jennifer. I was so panicked that I forgot that none of them was home. I was the only kid on the block who did not call for his mother when pain came calling.

I had been hit by two people. The first blow landed on my heart and was terrible; the second had absently glanced off my arm. I had not seen the blows coming because I was dramatically nearsighted. I used to think that punches were natural phenomena that just appeared, and came with your face, like bad breath in the morning.

When the second fist only made me cry louder, gurgling like a Listerine junkie, the group lost interest and passed on.

I knocked on my door. I rang the bell. I screamed loudly with enough heart to shatter panes in a glazier's shop. A disembodied voice filtered down to me from an upstairs window.

"I didn't whistle for you," it said.

I irritated someone else about an hour later, and discovered that screaming, crying, and making other disgusting, self-effacing noises were no bar to beating. In fact, they added spice.

"It hurt!" I cried, convinced that the punches would end if their sponsors understood that pain was the result.

The boys on the block were accustomed to blows and did not see them as cause for drama. My screams goaded them to greater effort. It opened no doors. I looked at my front door, the former gateway to sanctuary, the portal to safety, as if it had betrayed me.

The spirit of the door had changed, as had the spirit of my mother.

At first I thought I was being punished in a universal way for language incompetence. Stepmother Edna hated my dialect, which was at the me-Tarzan level, and it was unmistakably clear how the neighborhood children viewed my communication patterns.

They dubbed me "Yow!" Later, because even "Yow" did not fully express my Martian nature, they settled on China Boy. China, in our neighborhood, was more bizarre, more remote, than a distant planet.

I knew that China Boy was not intended as an affectionate moniker. I didn't get it. My family was Chinese, a fact of which they seemed proud.

"China Boy" sounded the dinner bell for a knuckle sandwich buffet. Being the China Boy outside the house was like being chum bait at a shark feed, an honor I could easily live without. In fact, I had to shed the honor before it consumed me.

I told Janie about the jungle outside our door. She had not been bothered by anyone in her long walk to the redbrick Roosevelt Junior High on Arguello. Her friends were in another neighborhood, one without a title, a nickname, a streetfighting ethic, or a death squad.

Why wasn't she China Girl? Why didn't they punch her nose and stand on *her* face?

"Ming-li. 'China Boy'—it bad name?" I asked.

"It's not good," she replied.

I thought about it.

"But I boy. From China. Sort of. I think."

She watched me leave our stoop for the street one day, seeing the kids gather around like a lynch mob after a child molester.

"Edna. Um, Stepmother. Please, Kai is really getting beaten up outside by all the street kids. He could really get hurt. He needs to be inside."

"Oh. *Well*," she said, the dual exclamations a promise of trouble. "He *needs* to be inside. How wonderful. He pesters me. He asks me questions I do not understand. He asks for food that Irish would not give to pigs. He looks like a refugee, and looks *stupidly* at *everything*. Now, he *needs* to be inside. What are *you*, Jane, his *mother*?

"Listen to me very carefully. You will interfere with my responsibilities regarding this very lost little boy only at supreme hazard to yourself. Do I make myself clear?"

She turned to me, hands on hips. "You are to remain in the street from the end of school until supper, and from after supper to bedtime. Out, now."

As I was being propelled again into my daily catastrophe on the sidewalk, Janie invited me to join her friends, north of the Panhandle.

Stepmother Edna said, "No. You belong on your own block, where I can whistle for you. You can't hear me on Encanto Way."

"No rike me, why make me be here?" I asked.

"Of course I don't dislike you. If you don't step outside *this* moment, you are going to be whipped silly."

Later, she told me that my father's job was so demanding, so hard, that he needed the comfort of his wife when he returned home.

"Seeing you and your sourpussed face only makes him sad," she said. "We are having a wonderful life, without you. You and your *sister*—" she said this as if it were a classic profanity—"are ruining it for us. You children are just *burdens*."

"Hello, darling," she breathed, as Father returned, taking his hat and acting as if the two of them were alone in the house.

I watched her sit before my mother's vanity. Edna was brushing her own hair. Mother seldom did this— it was my sisters' work. The light platinum of Edna's hair, undulating beneath the strokes of a golden brush,

enchanted me and I entered their room on silent feet
to sit behind her. I marveled at the nearness of her
size and shape to that of Mother. Now, at this moment, she did not seem like a *wupo*. I closed my eyes
and listened to the sound of her brush wisping through
her hair, taking comfort from hearing distantly familiar sounds from my stepmother without suffering in-
jury or fright. I think she knew I was there, but I was
never sure. After some minutes, I rose and left the
room.

Stepmother Edna was like a living statue, obviously
capable of all human activity, but limited for unclear
reasons to a restricted range of interaction. I had really
needed Mother, and then found myself wanting a
mother, any mother. I could tell that Edna thought I
was a bad, small person, probably of the wrong color,
undoubtedly of the wrong personality, operating badly
with the tongue of a monkey.

It was not her fault. She had not wanted us—her
connection was to Father. Nor had she wanted stepmother status any more than any rational person might.
She simply wanted a happy marriage.

I wanted to be a fighter pilot. With my eyesight, I
would have operated Thunderjets the way Mother had
driven Fords, but I would have crashed and burned in
the joy of flight. With Edna's sadness and anger, after
losing her husband to Chinese infantry in Korea, she
was not destined to be Mother of the Year in our once-
Asian household. While I understood none of this,
Edna was tied to the yoke of undesired motherhood.

It was her karma. My karma was to help her ex-
punge her personal devils by being smaller than she
was when she was angry.

Without running for office, I had been made the
Poster Boy for Corporal Punishment, enjoying all
rights and privileges thereto pertaining, and with all
fists, feet, bells, whistles, and sirens appropriate to the
station.

My youth seemed interminable because my personal

identity was unclear, and in the resulting fog the gauge of time became unmeasurable. Time seemed to lag because the neighborhood was committed to the idea of child warfare, and I was an early pacifist. My stepmother was an agent of emotional estrangement, of war by proxy, combat by youth, and chronic discipline.

I had embarked on my first rite of passage into boyhood, into violence and the realm of the fist.

6

REVOLUTION

While the manly stage of development on the street would last a decade, only the first year was dehumanizing. At home, however, the process of reconstruction began badly and soon worsened.

To an unformed child, Edna Madalyn McGurk Ting was like nuclear fusion. Awesome power, few controls, and no reasonable comprehension for the technically uninformed.

I think she liked me until she heard me speak, watched me walk, saw my clothing, observed my skinniness, and realized that I ate Chinese food willingly.

She had come from wealth and had mistaken Father's moneyed past as a precursor for the future. She had never before met a poor banker. We were waiting for a number of good things to happen, such as winning the Irish Sweepstakes or discovering uranium under the staircase. None of these events occurred. Edna pretended that they already had. She used denial the way Big Willie Mack used fists.

"Tell me again," she sighed languorously to my father, "about the servants who bathed your mother." Or about the live-in cook's family, the splendid fish cook, the live-in tailor who could fix Western watches. About the Sikh house constabulary, the personal maids, the servants who swept the outside verandas and journeyed to the burial grounds to sweep graves, the servants who stood silently against the walls of the dining room during meals, waiting to offer the gold tongue scrapers and gargling bowls before dessert, the *amahs* who tended the many raucous children of the Ting clan.

The geocultural distance between Shanghai and Philadelphia describes all the differences in the world, but she completely understood one major element in our domestic practice: the hallowed protection of family secrets.

When Stepmother Edna's younger sister Eileen visited us, I was instructed, "You will smile and obey me absolutely while Aunt Eileen is here. If you do not, if you show that dull, ugly, scowly little Asiatic expression in her presence I will make you sleep outside in the street and will tan your bottom black and blue."

She could not have learned to think like that at Smith.

When Aunt Eileen arrived with her family, Janie and I smiled like beauty-queen contestants until our faces ached. We were ready to do toothpaste ads for Ipana or Pepsodent.

"Don't you wish you looked like our cousin Kate?" I asked Janie. I had wanted to look black, but Eileen and Kate had more food, nicer clothes, and apparently had never been beaten.

"Shhh!" hissed Janie. "Speak in English! No! Why would I want to look like a *lo fan* ghost? Her hair is so light, it looks like it's not there." She paused.

"It's weird; Eileen doesn't seem anything like Edna. Something really bad must've happened to her."

True, I thought. Me.

"I am *so* lucky!" cried Edna to her sister. "These children are *wonderful*. They are the blessings of my life."

"See that you maintain this comportment at all times," she instructed after Eileen left.

To keep a secret, Edna sacrificed truth and took no prisoners.

"As far as anyone else is concerned, we are *not* poor. We are merely saving for future purchases."

I feel sympathy for her now, when my regrets can provide her no comfort, and the memory of my growing antipathy sits like corrosive guilt on the linings of my heart.

She expected to be the happy wife of a good lawyer, without any intent to have children. She instead became a lonely bereaved widow. Then she anticipated joining a sophisticated Chinese society family and living comfortably, and ended up in a mother role without the money, the temperament, or the training.

In making our family a victim of her cultural chauvinism, she administered a self-inflicted wound and denied herself the love and affection that could have been the sustenance of her life.

Father, known as the Colonel, was a celebrity of sorts in Chinatown. He was a decorated war hero, a former biplane fighter pilot, a paratrooper trained by the American army, an infantryman trained by the Germans. He worked for Madame Amethyst Jade Cheng, who had as much wealth as Croesus and whose parents had possessed impeccable political connections to Chiang Kai-shek. She had a deep, rich laugh that showed all her teeth. She was a free person, invigorated every day by the undeniable fact of her freedom, elevated by the inestimable breadth of her material wealth. She loved success, adored money, and learned charity. It was only the latter fact that drew my father to her in any personal way: charity was American.

I remember Madame Cheng as two people. First, as an alabaster goddess who was almost spritelike, a young woman prancing in the world of mature financiers, giggling as I and other young sons of her employees knelt and pressed our foreheads to the cold, red-tiled floor. Within the space of a few years, she had abandoned her ivory complexion for the burnished bronze of a frequent traveler to the south of France and would laughingly pull us to our feet whenever the kow tao seemed appropriate.

"Young gentlemen!" she said in her Shanghai-accented Mandarin. "You are Americans! Don't bow! Chew gum!" and she would laugh as she lifted her chin, her ebony-black, short-cropped, Dutch Boy coif falling back from her prominent forehead.

Father was poor, handsome, direct, and dashing. He was utterly unconventional. Father saw what had become of traditional Chinese values in the modern world. He had suffered the chaos, the irresponsibility, the waste, and the obsolescence of a culture that could not fashion an airborne corps, run a modern railway, operate a film industry, or defeat superstition.

His father, a friend of the poppy and an escort for concubines, a man who had not worked a day in his life, had been Chinese. My father was going to be American.

"We are in America!" he roared at his colleagues in the China Lights Bank, causing inkwells to jump and paper stacks to crash to the tiled floor.

"No more ancestor worship! No more stinking joss sticks! Firecrackers to chase spirits! No!! We should be celebrating Thanksgiving and Fourth of July! And memorizing goddamn Constitution! To form more perfect union, establish justice!"

So Father was in a unique position—a society notable whose rabid pro-Americanism placed him on the daring edge of the social register. Neo-hero, counter-culture rebel. A middle-aged Jimmy Dean.

The president of the bank was a hard-faced aesthete with cheekbones so deeply indented that he appeared skull-like under harsh ceiling lights. He had been a Cheng kinsman in the Su Sung Tai and had honorably carried a fourth of the wealth of the clan out of war-torn China to the Bank of England, in his patron's name. Amethyst Jade knew that Mr. Lew could have forgotten his duty and disappeared in storied opulence in Zurich. But he was the ultimate in loyalty, drawn to his boss by her entrepreneurial courage, her charismatic capitalism. He was also amused by Father's unconventionality, and clearly marveled at him for his lack of focus on wealth. I think he regarded the marriage to Edna McGurk as a supreme coup, since Edna looked like the women who made movies in Hollywood and advertised kitchen soaps in the magazines. But there were some in the community who did not share his cosmopolitanism.

When the later woes of the China Lights Bank became common knowledge, Edna discovered that we were genuinely poor.

Victoria Lum Ting, one of the powers in the local family association, visited our house. She made a point of speaking to all of us in Songhai, and dealing with Edna as if she were the village idiot. Victoria, who had all the compassion of a toad after flies, knew that Father's fortune was waning while her wealth increased. The word was out on Grant Avenue: Amethyst Jade is restructuring and will base her operations henceforth in Singapore and Hong Kong. All staff who wish can follow. Those who stay possess their own joss.

"Edna, would you want to live in Singapore?" asked Father.

"Oh, darling, you can't be serious!" she exclaimed. "The communists would *love* to take Singapore. It fell to the Japanese in—hours! You can't possibly want me to be so close to the Reds!"

Victoria wore her most sumptuous mink coat, her fingers winking with every diamond ring she could borrow from the Ying Yum Jewelry Mart. Victoria's rude demeanor did not promise improved East–West relations.

"Ah ha, Ting Taitai," said Victoria. "You like mink, or you like sable? Thank golly my husband, when he alive, no put his money in China Lights Bank! So, you think go, Singapore? Ha-ha. Nice ring, ehah?"

So my pushing and hustling for Chinese food in what was regarded as a hostile tongue must have set the worst possible tone for positive coexistence. The sound of the Chinese language had become Edna's talisman for poverty, exclusion, isolation.

This set up the Sunday punch. This was the Western world, where to spare the rod was to spoil the child. On the other hand, the Chinese think that if you continually beat a youngster or slap him in the face his brains will seep through his ears. And you will be rewarded in later years with someone who fires burning arrows into everyone's barns.

"Why must you make those terrible faces at me when I tell you to do something?" she asked.

I struggled for the words.

"You're frowning again!" Stop that! said her hand against my cheek. The nonverbal tradition of the family was being upheld.

She discovered that fate had rendered her a missionary, tasked with the salvation of a heathen band of lost souls, without offerings at the altar or solace in the prayers. Missionaries should have willing flocks. It is tough to reform something that is shapeless and indifferent to improvement, like Jell-O in the hands of a carpenter.

We had lost our cultural glue in the Run. The keepers of the flame of custom were dead, absent, or in college.

Edna McGurk valued the suburban look. This was the ascent of the Golden Fifties, when *Good Housekeeping* was more than a magazine and the concept was grander than a golden seal. Suburban thinking was in vogue, but totalitarianism was better. It was also more affordable.

"Sit up taller. Put your knife on the back of the plate. Keep the napkin square on your lap or it will fall off, and you may not drop anything on the floor. Cut small pieces and chew methodically with your mouth *totally* closed. No speaking at the dinner table. Elbows off, wipe your mouth." There was much to learn.

Whipped by bad fortune, surrendering to the inexorable gravity of downward-sliding consequences, Edna enforced home order without compromise. Discipline was the staff of life. It became our true religion, more impressive than the magical fries in the Lew Wallace Eatery, more eloquent than the heavenly chorus in the neighborhood Holy Christian Church of Almighty God.

But the application of discipline was uneven. Edna was intimidated by Jennifer and Megan's maturity, and they were in college at Cal. Jennifer Sung-ah was studying music; Megan was in education. Jennifer liked Edna because she was smart and honest. Megan liked Edna because she did not torture her, as our mother had.

Jennifer could have outwitted Einstein and was the safest from Edna's interference. That left the short sprouts of Janie and me. Edna was not reluctant to beat us for an endless series of capital transgressions, usually involving facial expressions, illegally spoken Chinese, poor table manners, and miserable carping about being slapped, hit, and kicked, in that order.

I had never been hit before. I think my sisters used to squeeze my arms or other appendages when my crying became insufferable, but face-slapping was not appropriate. Nor was kicking. Or punching.

The first time Stepmother Edna hit me I was convinced it was a mistake and waited dumbly for an apology. She was waiting for mine. When I realized that she *meant* to hit me, I trembled and let loose the tears of the Last Flood. Edna discovered, to her surprise, that more, emphatic hitting did not terminate my crying. I felt pain, outrage, more pain, hot anger. Then, a flat disassociation. I am not here, I said, limiting my involvement in the world to the range of my myopic eyes. Edna wondered if I was retarded, but the thought was not enough to save me.

Megan hinted that slapping children in the face was not Chinese.

"We are *not* in China, Megan," Edna would say through her teeth. "That is precisely the point I am striving to make."

Then Janie announced that if Edna ever touched her again, she would kill her. Janie had turned fourteen without a party, a noisemaker, or a hot cup of tea. She looked twelve, and had been as innocent as Mary's little lamb. Like all children, she was not inherently violent; she was adapting to the culture of her home. We thought we were becoming European.

"How would you kill her?" I whispered in Songhai while Janie read the Hunan chopsticks story to me.

"I will drive the *chi tz*, the car, and run over her," she said. I nodded. That idea made sense. We respected driving as others regarded natural catastrophes.

Edna figured she could not afford to call Janie's bluff. After all, what if she meant it? So I became the sole target of corporal punishment. I was beginning to see a global purpose to Edna's plan. Beat him on the inside, whip him on the outside, and pretty soon he'll cooperate and tell us everything. You know, spill the beans.

I just couldn't figure out what the information was.

Edna stormed me with words—an incessant, articulate torrent of elevated vocabulary uttered with careful diction and unmistakable menace. My ears began to ring in response to her anger. I did not understand her, and she could barely tolerate me.

But her true weapons were emotional. Oh, Kai, did you not pick up your room? Fine. See this model airplane? Crunch! It was a balsa Curtis P-40 Tomahawk, carefully completed just a few days before. Is this your creamed corn unfinished on the plate? Very well, no dinner tomorrow, and I will take your firetruck away. Take that look off your face! Slap! Crunch! to the firetruck, and Smash! again as it resists her stomps. Whap, I told you to keep your elbow from the table. I gave you three minutes to be in the bathroom and you have taken four. Kick. You did not move your bowels at 7:30 as I instructed. How else can you become regular? Kick. Oh, you did not go to sleep as directed, at eight? Slap. Very well. You may not speak to Jane for one day. Your clothes look terrible, almost as bad as you, be that possible. I don't care how it happened. Don't make that face! Slap!

I watched her destroy my toys, numb in the face of loss and helpless in the tide of history.

Janie stood up to Edna, and was rewarded with progressively worsening life conditions.

"Edna, would I be able to invite Donna Riley over?" she asked. Janie did not look at our stepmother, controlling her face.

"Please address me, Jane, as 'Stepmother Edna.' "

"Stepmother Edna. Can Donna Riley visit?"

"When?" asked Edna.

"Whenever. This weekend?"

"No," said Stepmother Edna.

"Some other time, then?"

Edna did not answer.

Edna provided me two gifts. The first was respite from peanuts. Mother's conditioning had worked; when I ate them, I became violently ill. Edna hated acceding to my weaknesses, but she hated the consequences of forcing her way with peanuts. The other gift was allowing me to keep my blankie, the one positive fugitive from the law of averages and an enduring survivor from the forces of assimilation. I looked at my blankie with hope; if it could survive, then so might I.

7

WATER

Our home was linguistically disarrayed. We sounded like elevator talk in the Tower of Babel, with a smorgasbord of Chinese dialects on the ground floor, a solid base in Songhai, a strong layer of Mandarin, and a smattering of *sam yep* Cantonese veneered on the top. Ascending, we found Father's unique hybrid blend of Chinese, English, and German accents employed in his pronunciation of English. Then came Jennifer and Megan's high English aristocratic accents—the products of Tutor Luke's original instruction and the year of speaking Empire English in India. Of course, had we been at the fount of the tongue, in Great Britain, their speech would have represented the apex. But this was America, and Janie's rapid grasp of American dialogue placed her just beneath the perfect enunciation of Edna, who rested at the pinnacle. My gibberish of eclectic sounds was actually not part of the structure and lay in the subbasement, in the antediluvian terrain of cavedweller grunting.

When Kaiser Wilhelm II lost the Great War, the Allies at Versailles demobilized the German Army. That was so the Germans would never make war again in

Europe, which reveals the practical value of political science. Chiang Kai-shek then hired three thousand unemployed German officers and NCOs as cadre for his Kuomintang Army. This was the China Military Mission, headed by the brilliantly capable General Hans von Seekt, a man my father admired despite his lack of American citizenship. Von Seekt was a professional, what the U.S. Army called a Regular.

Thus, before Pearl Harbor brought America into the war, Father had been trained for battle by the kaiser's veterans in North China. They taught in the universal language of war: military English, with a German dash, a monocled eye, and artillery, which is globally understood.

We had the customs of a family uprooted from its ethnoculture and dropped on its head in the wrong neighborhood in the wrong country. We should have gone to Germany. I still wanted to go to Tsingtao, and I didn't even like beer.

Edna knew that we, like the soldiers of Bonaparte, lived on our stomachs. The heart of the matter, in a Chinese household, is food.

How are you? ask the French and other Latins. Americans ask: How's it going? Tibetans say, I pray for you. The Chinese ask: Have you eaten? So Edna found our Achilles heel—in the abdomen.

Janie had become a great cook and provided us pleasure in her meals. But that was now *finis*. Behind Edna's Irish roots lay three things: potatoes, a German maid, and an unconscious dislike of cooking. I called potatoes *Dai-fan*, or Big Rice Kernel. Janie called sauerkraut "rotted pig poop."

Bye-bye, food. Bye-bye mu shu pork.
Hello, cauliflower, I think I'm gonna die.
Bye-bye, sweet food, good-bye.

Jennifer and Megan's visits home on weekends became infrequent.

I began staring at mirrors, wondering what it was in my face that made Stepmother Edna so violent, so angry. Edna's cultural offensives were launched when our defenses were weakest—at dinner. Communication to Janie and me arrived with the boiled squash in the presence of our father. Her pronouncements were delivered with the formality of a Vatican edict. Edna attacked the incomprehensible gibberish of the house.

"We are only to speak English henceforth," she announced. "Absolutely *no* Chinese, in any form. The removal of this *foreign* food will help, since I understand that no proper words exist to describe it.

"Kai, that means no singing songs in Chinese. Jane, that means that you will say nothing behind my back that I cannot understand. There will be no breaching of this policy."

"What," asked Jane, who had the courage of Daniel, "will Father do when Uncle Shim or Mr. Soo Hoo call from the bank, and he has to talk to them in Songhai?"

"Your father's conversations are private. Besides, that is not Chinese. That is banking.

"Furthermore. 'Uncle Shim' is *not* your uncle. And he calls this house too frequently. He has such a curious voice. That reminds me. Why, sweetheart," she asked Father, "does this Mr. Shim want to call so often?"

"Darling, he's a friend, as good as Na-men, uh, Norman Schwatz'd," he replied, still daunted by the linguistic pretzel of Na-men's name. "His family know my family in China. Shim is a top scholar, very, very smart. He, uh, teach Kai how to write Chinese."

"Well, obviously, *that* must stop! Your son must be *American*, and not be confused by conflicts in culture!"

Clothes were next. She dressed Jane in rags to make her look bad to establish clearly the undesirability of another female in the house. Our family was the only one I knew that had designated two separate daughters as Cinderellas, under different mothers. Edna dressed me in Little Lord Fauntleroy outfits to make me look good. In our neighborhood, it was pinning a bright red bull's-eye on a sitting duck. Kids who want to live to morning recess do not wear blue velvet outfits with white neck-buttoned shirts. I could not have done worse if I had worn a placard saying, SCREW ALL YO' MOMMAS, TWICE.

Eventually, economics saved me. Little Lord clothing was costly, and it was being trashed by my community beatings as soon as the tailoring was complete. Edna stopped buying such clothes for a while. This did not stop my daily cultural goofs and the resulting creamings, but it saved me from poundings by kids from other neighborhoods who saw me for the first time from across the schoolyard.

Once, as I was fleeing some street bullies, I sprinted past my own door and saw that it had been left ajar. Edna went out no more frequently than my mother, but she must have cracked the door for a look and forgotten to lock it. Feeling the luck of the Irish, I braked hard, jammed inside and latched the door, panting. Edna appeared immediately and forced me outside with paddling hands and helping feet.

"I hate you!" I cried, as the pack closed in.

She hit me so hard with an open palm to my face that the herd stopped, incredulous that the pretty blonde had done its work. For free. The blinding violence of her hand was so public, the shattering impact of her blow so immediate, that I felt my spirit blanch in panicked retreat. My sense of internal self evaporated and my brain rocked as tiny lancets of ice-white light sprinkled across my optic field.

That night she whacked me with a belt.

"You *never* tell your *mother* that you *hate* her!" she cried, her belt singing. "Only little beasts, *animals,* say things like that! And that is what you *are!*"

"You not my mah-mee!" I wailed with desperate logic.

The beating worsened, frightening me more with her fury than the actual blows, which alone were crowding my screaming panic with the fear that she would not stop.

"Arguing won't help," she hissed, panting with her effort. "I *am* your mother. By God, it is the best thing that ever happened to you! If you knew how corrupt your illiterate mother was! You will know this someday, and regret this horrid, devillike resistance to me! Can you do nothing about that morbid, defiant face!"

Therein lay a fundamental problem: animals versus her unique interpretation of Philadelphia Society. Edna wanted meals to resemble the paintings of Rembrandt—silent, stately, admirable, full of shadow and tint, and quietly aesthetic.

The Chinese eat with the joy of abandonment, the relish of a pride of lions. The object of a Chinese meal is eating. It is not a spectator sport, and the theme of the exercise is free pleasure after a long day's work. Chinese food is complex artistry in preparation, and simple, unrestrained celebration in eating. People talk, shout, laugh, and enjoy what must modestly be viewed as the most complex and diverse cuisine in the world.

The Chinese are smart; they reserve aristocratic airs for the business of court and permit the child within us all to romp freely with happy little chopsticks at dinnertime.

Edna must have viewed her first meal in our home in nauseous dismay, a rapid descent into Dante's kitchen. The snuffling, the talking with food in the mouth, the elbows on the table, the unknown taxonomy of the strange things on people's plates probably had the same effect on her as a Milk of Magnesia–and-mustard-based emetic.

The purpose of a meal with Edna was protocol. We learned an elaborate preparatory procedure that made scrubbing for brain surgery seem dilatory. No talking, no grinning. Death to laughers. Food to a fascist is somber business. After all, it eventually produces waste matter. Unless no one eats.

Chairs just so. No wrinkles in the tablecloth. Without funds, we purchased silver and glassware. Knife first at your right, water glass centered on its tip, one inch away. Water in each glass two inches from the lip. Dinner fork, left, napkin artfully displayed. Knife, spoon. On left and right, outside, like tackles in a standard pro-set, were salad fork and soup spoon.

"Salad forks on the *outside*!"

A bloodcurdling scream would issue forth, then a sharp slap on the cheek would bring all the blood in the body into the face.

We never saw a salad and had little soup. But the utensils were patiently in attendance, in case the missing victuals were airdropped by the 82d Airborne or Mr. Campbell Soup visited without calling first.

The marks of childhood endure. Today, when I see silverware improperly aligned, I feel a jab of fright, a small, tender sliver of pain, a threat of disorder and possible doom.

We prayed.

Mother had joined the Episcopalian Church in prewar Shanghai when she realized that daily missionary English lessons were part of the deal. She loved learning, and English seemed so much the vogue. My father often spoke of Rice Christians—that is, Chinese who accepted the teachings of missionaries in return for the meals. I understood that. Mother had been a Keats Christian, a Dickensian parishioner, a Shakespearean Follower of Jesus, enduring the Old Testament for lessons in the new tongue of English, the language of new-age Chinese college students, the currency of the brave new world.

The missionaries could have laughed last, had that derisive sentiment been in them. When Mother arrived in America and realized the distance from China, her family, and her father, and that the passing fancy of British words was now the dominant tongue of her physical world, she began attending church regularly, asking God's forgiveness for past insincerities. But she resented the tongue. It was a reminder of her losses.

Now Jane Ming-li had assumed the role of conscience in our mother's absence, and tried to find an explanation for Edna in every book in the Bible. We both were fascinated with Exodus. Megan Wai-la, abandoned by our mother and seemingly by the gods, was understandably drawn to agnosticism. Jennifer Sung-ah, like our mother, adored Mozart. Father was a Confucian, which is a nonsecular ethical faith and involves ancestor rituals inappropriate for the dinner table.

Edna was an eclectic adventurer in religion. Except for Episcopalianism, she never met a faith she did not like. Her present passion was Christian Science, and she was unsure of its blessings before meals, so she directed us all to pray individually. Edna's religious adventures were vicarious, for her explorations meant that someone else would be the dutiful pilgrim attending services. She never went.

I did. Edna had sent me to the Holy Christian Church of Almighty God—a place I found by location and not by name recognition—and anxiety pressed on me as everyone under the roof sang their hearts out in mind-sweeping melodic majesty. When I first heard the rich, emotive singing, I did not realize that the people in the congregation were producing it. Nor did I know the words, except for ''Jesus'' and ''love,'' but the huge crescendo of feelings—of safety, and caring—that rushed through my small body made me weep. Somehow I knew that I could cry in these pews without fear and without shame. Others, taller and older than I, also wept.

Reverend Stamina Jones was a tall, stately, white-haired man with clear eyes in an extremely dark round face. His voice was so low that it tickled my tailbone. He had a softness to him that made men open their hands and surrender their fists. He ministered with a capability as deep and wide as his voice, singing the song of love.

I reminded myself that Mother had attended an Episcopalian Church in China, as well as in the City, and I imagined her strong musical voice in the choir, singing, secretly, for Na-Gung.

But of all the churches I attended—Methodist, Community, Apostolic, Baptist, Foursquare Gospel, and Catholic—the most unique was the Church of Christian Science. It was the Ninth Church of Christ Science on Junipero Serra Boulevard—named after the famous Catholic friar—in the all-Anglo mansion district of St. Francis Woods. This was just two miles from Ocean Beach, with its diagonal and perpendicular parking slots that had always confounded Mother. Four blocks away was Sigmund Stern Grove, where the parks department presented free summer Sunday concerts and Pine Lake was stocked with fish for the children to catch.

In the Handle, we had Fist City concerts and nocturnal meetings of the Righteously Pissed Males' Knife and Gun Club, and the streets were stocked with broken people.

In the Ninth Church, I was the only nonwhite. I was openly accepted, though no one had a clue from whence I had come. Edna said that she had picked the Christian Scientists for me because the founder was a woman, and because it seemed that the faith was premised on strength of belief. I suspect that the true reason was that St. Francis Woods was far away and provided another automatic day when I would be gone. She had given me the directions and I had left, taking buses like a maestro of the Municipal Railway. I sat quivering in the back of the Church.

I worried when everyone turned whisperingly to stare, the sound of bottoms twisting on wooden pews accentuating the words of the minister. I looked behind me to see a pure white wall. But I was not scared and my legs did not tense with the need for flight. I did not smell that biting, salivating mob drive that communities often generate when people of the wrong club enter without invitation. No fascists, stepmothers, or rabid dogs here.

It was safe and ordered. The organ music was beguiling, and probably matched the gothic horror of our home. The singing was much quieter, more subdued, less motivating than the congregation's work in the Holy Christian Church. My body did not keep rhythm with the hymns by crying, and Jesus did not move me. The music was exterior to me. People seemed to be holding on, not letting go. They were protecting something, and I did not know what it was.

After the subdued service, which was no more understandable than Reverend Jones's, a man in a light tan suit approached.

"Bob Lamport," he said, offering his hand. I shook it.

"What's your name, young man?"

"China Boy Kai Ting," I said, as honestly as I could. A hesitation.

"What shall I call you?"

I shrugged. I was trying to think that names were not so important.

"May I call you Kai?"

I nodded.

"Let me take you to Sunday School. I'm one of the teachers."

He led me from the pew to a side room, separated by a clean, deep blue curtain. Blond, blue-eyed children were seated in the room, and Mr. Lamport introduced me to them.

These kids were like Kate Potts, Aunt Eileen's daughter. They were dressed like royalty and were as orderly as a drill team in final competition. They were chubby and unbruised.

The Sunday School lesson dealt with Joseph's coat of many colors. The story involved brothers killing each other.

A girl with hair the color of sunlight, wearing clothes from *T'ien*, Heaven, played the organ, and I had the same magnetic pull to her as I did to Anita Mae Williams, a stunning older girl in the Handle whose face was so pretty it made me feel weak. I loved the blond girl in some strange and inexplicable way, watching her fingers make the music my mother would have adored.

The kids in the Ninth Church had mastered life itself.

The organ player said good morning to me, and I pretended that I was deaf, staring straight ahead, filled with hope and fear. I am not sure what Mary Baker Eddy thought of the outcome; I knew with every fiber of my being that Christian Science could not alter the sum and substance of Edna's kicks or Big Willie's fists. But I got to travel on Sundays.

I was facing daily death in the streets and was the only true believer at the dinner table. I needed to have faith in a merciful God, knowing that he was keeping score, and that I had not been doing well. I needed help. I wanted my mother to return. I prayed to Him with a zeal that wrinkled my brows, drew most of my forehead into my eye sockets, and worried casual observers.

We endured all of this for fresh breadsticks, boiled cabbage, flinty lima beans, hardy brussels sprouts, and undercooked hamburger stew. Edna loved to have a carefully set table. She hated to cook, for it had been an unlearned skill in a house with a live-in German maid. I missed Mother's burnt toast.

Edna did not do these things to make us miserable. Well, she did them to make Janie miserable, but she merely wanted to improve the home.

"Janie," said Edna. "When you learn to enjoy brussels sprouts, I will allow you to buy that dress at Sears."

"It's gone," said Janie. "The sale ended months ago, and it's not on the rack."

"Well. It was very ugly. Because you have black hair, there's little you can wear. As I said, when you *like* brussels sprouts, if you do not criticize me again, I will look for another. Meanwhile, I am taking away your green coat, as a reminder of your responsibilities to be respectful to your family."

"I don't care!" cried Janie, running headlong into the maw of the consuming enemy.

"Very well," replied Edna. "Then I will take your poodle skirt."

"That's not mine! It's Margaret Apodaca's!" she wailed.

Worse for Edna, however, than the brooding resentment over the slapping, kicking, and hitting, the food revolution, the loss of possessions, the religious reformation, the casting out of tongues, the ancient art of German clothing torture, and the onset of team depression was the lingering memory of the first Mrs. Ting.

Mother's presence was palpable. We could hear her voice, her call to spirits, her effervescent laughter; we could smell the memory of joss sticks and her hundreds of matches to ignite the paste. We stared at the empty bathtub, the toaster, the clocks, and touched the steering wheel of the 1950 Ford as if the fervor of our eyes could animate her return. I would rub the bedspread where she sat when she read to me, holding the books, carving into my memory the texture of her caressing voice. I felt the warm slenderness of her patrician fingers as they traced the characters in her tutor's book, their special spirit shimmering in my immature memory.

Janie Ming-li and I looked out the attic window to the ocean, where I thought she might be visiting. I always peered for her at the beach, my heart racing if I saw a running figure.

"Don't you think," Edna asked brightly at one of our customary funerallike medieval dinners, "that Dai-li was a *terrible* mother?"

"She wasn't so bad," offered Megan, who was visiting and the only one at the table who could have honestly agreed with the question.

I smelled smoke, and for one thrilling moment I thought it was Mother making toast in the kitchen. But once seated, we could not move.

"Janie. Mommy at toaster?" I asked.

Janie looked at me as if I had asked her if she were Bob Hope. But when she looked into the kitchen and didn't shout for joy, I knew that something other than toast was burning.

"Your mother," said Edna, "was *also* a terrible cook."

The normal hush at the table was replaced by a silence that every mother of newborn triplets prays for, and never receives.

"Her very moral fiber was rotten to the core. She had *servants* cook her meals in China. *This* is America," she said slowly, "where individual dignity is a hallowed principle."

Please, Janie, I thought, don't mention Stepmomma Edna's German cook. Arguing won't help.

"For which good men have died."

She was referring to her first husband. I thought she was speaking about me.

I was cutting up the sauerkraut to hide it under the liver. I tasted the liver and shuddered, storing it in a corner of my cheek. Then I tried to hide the liver under the sauerkraut, wondering how I could empty my mouth. Early Rubik's Cube.

"Edna," said Megan, "you should ask Jane that question."

I looked up. Megan had not lived with Edna. No, no. *Don't* ask Janie what she thinks! Edna will hear her answer!

Jane's face illuminated, and she said, in a big rush, "She was a *wonderful* Mom. She *loved* us. She *fed* us and didn't beat us and she let us sing. She would never slap . . ."

"Silence!" cried Edna as she sprang from her seat and slapped Jane, and I involuntarily jumped, catapulting a hideous piece of liver across the table, splatting it onto the silver butter dish, which was always empty. But clean.

I expected death. I had few toys left. I wondered if Janie, her face livid with the mark of Edna's hand, was going to drive the Ford into the dining room and flatten Edna into the pancake she was striving to form from me.

"Henceforth, there will be *no mention* of Dai-li," Edna screamed like a priest in a whorehouse.

"I have taken the photo albums that she dragged here from China and *burned* them! I burned the whole crate they were in! All that trash is now *smoke*! This is America! And *she does not exist*!" She was standing, stamping her feet on the floor.

"This hurts my feet!" she cried.

Everyone screamed but me. My father swore. The crate contained some of his identity papers, photos and letters from war buddies, his old uniforms, and Sam Browne belts.

"Goddamn!" he roared. "There was live .38 Super ammo in box! It could have cooked off and killed *everyone*! Why not *ask* first!"

"Because you would have said no!" she yelled back.

For years, my sisters' friends did not believe this story. "Incredible," they would say. "Impossible!" they would exclaim. "She *couldn't*!" they would cry.

Our mother's wedding gown had been in the crate and my sisters expected to use it someday. My sisters' proof of Edna's spectacular act of cultural violence was the absence of the famous gown on each of their marriage days. I know that my sisters cried at their weddings, and I at first thought it was because of our stepmother's arson.

The albums were Jennifer's favorite possessions in the world, but this night she had chosen the dust of the Cal library over liver and sauerkraut. She was spared the trauma of dinner, the object lesson in human dignity, and the smoke of Revolution.

I must have looked too calm, for Edna looked at me with wild eyes, pointing a finger that seemed to have the friendliness of a Flash Gordon death ray.

"Dai-li Ting is *dead*!! What a stupid secret to keep!" she cried. "And don't think I didn't know about those filthy foreign books! And those awful Chinese pens and dirty inks! They were in the crate, too!" That made me join in the community cry. So much for Uncle Shim's treasured calligraphy, the notions of Santa Claus, the domestic gods of our kitchen, and *The Tales of Lu Hsun*.

"Stop it!" she shrilled at our orchestra of wails.

My father rose and left the table. I wished he had asked me to join him. His departure was dignified, orderly, and sensible.

Whenever Mother had severely criticized Megan Wai-la, Father was at work. My worst beatings by Edna occurred when he was overseas, at the bank, or at meetings. This was Woman's Work.

I felt the imbalance in duties, the unfairness of responsibility, but it was the best argument I knew for possessing the status of a grown man.

The crying stopped, the sniffling and nose-blowing began.

"Mah-mee alive, not dead," I said to myself, my hands between my legs, rocking back and forth, again and again that night. I sat up in my bed until dawn, my mind and legs aching, unable to sleep, wanting to turn on all the lights in the house, knowing I lacked the authority. Mother had loved electricity.

I comforted myself with Reason. Ma-ma had brought my sisters out of wartime China. She used to throw knives at bad guys and could live with communists and survive the attacks of warlord *ping*. She was still practicing knife-throwing, in Tsingtao. She never gave up. She would never give up, would not give me up. Nor

Father. Nor Jennifer, nor Janie. Maybe Megan. But not me.

I followed my father into the bathroom the next morning.

"Ma-ma dead, Baba?" I asked in a whisper, fearing suspicious spirits, listening gods, and Edna. I knew then that it would be okay if he didn't answer.

He lowered his head into his hands, fingers rasping whiskers. He raised his head up slightly, and brought it down decisively, his lips tight, bloodless. Yes. And now we have said it.

"Cancer. Cancer killed her," he said in the voice of a small mouse.

"Who Cancer, Baba?" I asked.

"Cancer is a disease," he said.

"Like god? Cancer god?" I asked.

He nodded. "Yes. The Cancer God." It was the only time that Father acknowledged the existence of spirits.

The rest of that week and that month became a blur of weeping, of my body becoming one of the base elements. Mother had been earth; I was becoming water.

I surrendered to emotional rages that lacked genesis and closure, blurred memories of beatings sparked by failed tasks and violations of Edna's protocols. I uttered spontaneous Chinese phrases, sent heated prayers to all authorities, and tried to understand the logic of Mother's death. I recited the Sixteen Edicts of Confucian Thought, tripping and stumbling awkwardly in Songhai, softly moaning with the realization that my native speech was becoming unfriendly, sliding out of the reach of my tongue. What would Uncle Shim say? Uncle Shim missing. Not even phone calls anymore. Father, going to Hong Kong next week, to be gone for two weeks. Then to Singapore.

Death, like in China. Finality. The Good-bye Forever. No Mother. You have a mother. A new mother.

The first one is gone, for all time, and your vital essence, your *shigong,* has followed her.

Sometime in that first week, or the second, following our Banquet of the Burning Crate, I tried to run away.

I was caught in the stairway by Edna. I had one worn blanket, an extra set of underwear, a broken flashlight, and twenty cents. I had no plan, no vision, no concept of where to go. I just wanted to be somewhere else.

I lost the last of my toys.

I could not sleep. The thought of my mother not returning made my body thrash on the bed in an agony of failed denial.

She is in Tsingtao with Na-Gung, Maternal Grandfather, and the two of them are playing with yellow fish while Wang the fish cook laughs until tears sparkle in his eyes.

They are preparing a place for me and Janie and I will learn music and be a *chien shur* scholar and will relearn Songhai and I will never do anything that could make her leave me again.

8

DOG MEAT

"Catch, China Boy!" shouted Tyrone Sykes as an antipersonnel grenade disguised as a rubber kickball caromed off my head.

"You sucka!"

The abuse inside the house was being reenacted by different players back on the street. The following months were filled with dramatizations of my almost universal incompetence. Three main areas of cultural failure appeared, refusing to be corrected by my merely being on the street.

First was language. My speech was bonkers. I lacked the words, the pronunciation, and the body language. My voice resembled marble-mouthed Esperanto chants. I lacked the thoughts that precede speech. I was too far behind to close the cultural gap by osmosis. I was like a water-skier without the skis, dragged through the wake of an uncompromising culture by my neck. I missed the nuances and the signals that accompany social existence in any milieu.

I didn't know what the kids in my neighborhood talked about for nearly a year. When I found out, I was disappointed; they discussed fighting and sports.

"Reginald, he beat tar outa dat cat from da Haight," said one.

"Nuh-uh!" said another. "Reginald, he tore inna dat boy, but he loss all his blood. Dat boy from da Haight? He a muthafucka, I promise you dat, and no Reginald no how got no chance wif him! Ya'll see da *guns* on dat boy? Reginald, he skinny lika rail! He dog meat!"

"Reginald, he dun *thump* dat boy. You lissena me!"

"Reginald, shee-it! No way! Dog meat, boy!"

"Naah. Is not!"

"Yeah! Is!"

"Is not, and da Yankees, dey gonna win jus like Reginald, an' make yo' ma'fuckenDahjers dog meat, too!"

I wanted to talk about food and hear about their mothers.

"Who ma'fucken?" I asked.

"China Boy," said one, tiredly. "Don be buttin in, fool. Don hurt yo mouf when ya'll don know *shit.*"

"Name Kai, no China Boy," I said accurately. "I from China," which was untrue. I was from the Panhandle.

Second was sports. The kids in the Handle played ball and fought. They ran, they jumped, they argued. They laughed. I understood the running part, but it brought me neither honor nor status.

After my peers had been born and weaned, round spherical bouncing objects had been placed in their hands until the relationship between them and the balls became a unity. I met my first ball at the age of seven. I discovered that it was a slippery reptile that came at high speed to smack me in my face without notice. It cleverly went left if I went right, went up when I went down. My swearing in Chinese at the cursed sphere did not seem to help. The ball became my enemy and made me the Martian the kids already suspected me to be.

The third area was the bottom line. Fighting was

the final test of life on the street. It measured a boy's courage and tested the texture of his guts, the promise of his nascent manhood, his worthiness to live and bear friends on poor streets. It was the ultimate *chien shur* examination, for instead of merely facing the Emperor, one faced himself.

Kids who could play ball but were chicken fighters did not belong on the block. They were supposed to stay in their homes. Kids who could do neither did not belong in the *world*, and were supposed to be banned, killed, or worse.

It took little time to discover that I was in a new category. I was the kid who knew nothing, played ball like a goat, had no fighting spirit and less ability, and would not stay in his house, leave the block, or die. Edna had locked the door and kept me within a whistle's reach.

The kids, too numerous to remember or name, tested me, hoping for a real fight, searching for evidence that I was human or that I possessed human potential. I occasionally swore in Chinese, which showed defiance to Edna. It inspired derisive laughter and never improved my station.

I responded to the challenge of combat with the tactics of avoidance and flight. The flights of the China Boy worked with the marketing aplomb of the Edsel.

I would try to elude notice, but I stood out like a white rat at a tomcat convention. A cultural gaffe would invite a pounding. I wouldn't say hello; I did say hello. I was sneaking around; I was strutting too proud. I didn't return a ball, or I touched a bruiser's holy kickball when I didn't have a right to. I took cuts like a girl; I made a face when called a name. Then Jerome, Jerue, Keith, James, J.T., Tyrone, Maurice, Big Willie, or Wally Junior would be in my face. A push on my chest, which, because of its limited area, required great accuracy.

Hey, I would squeak, unconvincingly, my head bouncing in whiplash.

There were about a dozen who got into the ritual of having the China Boy for lunch. Or, if I were really slow that day, for breakfast. I was sunshine Wheaties for an entire generation of future boxers.

Jerue had to push four times and recite a litany of four epic profanities involving my mother before he kicked for the groin. He liked to keep the banquet to one course. Keith Scott was the opposite, never quite sure how he would start, focusing on dessert, when he would finish with certain foot stomps. Reginald Tufts, whose fighting ability was frequently the topic of heated debate, hit me until I cried. I learned to cry quickly with him, and we were both satisfied.

Some kids gave two pushes, some five, building up. But protocol called for the opening push, like soup before the main course. Then a fist, then two. First the arm, then the gut, then the face. Sometimes a kick. Each tormentor had his habit.

Jerome was like the Twelve Celestial Heavens full-course Chinese banquet. He would scream obscenities, loud enough to scare me half to death just by the sound of them. Then a push on the chest, followed by punches and *then* kicking.

J.T. had a push that knocked me into next week. He'd laugh, which was worse than the physical hurt, for it imprinted itself on the brain longer than muscle could hold a bruise, and that, with the long-lasting memories of his heckling giggle, was the fight. And so on.

As my concrete internship gained momentum, Father drove me to Big Recreational Field in the park, known as Big Rec. He parked and when I got out he was holding two baseball mitts and a hardball. I put the small glove on. Instead of descending into the bowl of the field itself, which was filled with Little Leaguers, we stayed on the bike path, next to the curb. He backed away, and I winced as the ball hit my chest.

''Bring glove up, catch ball,'' he said.

I smiled, found the ball, and rolled it back to him.

Once again the ball arrived from nowhere in particular, to hit me on the arm. It stung a little. Again, I smiled, wishing Father had brought calligraphy instead of ball torture. Four or five times later, the ball hit me on the shoulder and rolled down a storm drain. Quietly, Father retrieved my mitt, put both of them in the trunk, and drove us home. I knew something had just happened, and that it was neither positive for our relationship nor good for my karma. I knew he was trying to reach me and that I was slipping away from him. I loved him so much for trying, hoping that the ball had not cost too much money and that the gloves could be returned.

"You need to be in good physical shape in America," he said. "Try to practice catch."

"Tyrone," said Maurice. "We be bashin China Boy from da get-go an he ain't laid a lick on us. Le's fuck dis shit an leave da slanteye sucka be."

"Dat who we *be*! We be da *Bashers*!"

When a group organized around torment gives itself a name, bad things can only worsen. I knew who the first Grand Poo-Bah of the China Boy Bashers was going to be. It was the Honorable Willis "Fist-In-Your-Face" Mack.

Big Willie was the worst of an evil band. He kicked and usually punched, but his size and strength produced blows that jarred the body and caused lapses in consciousness. He fought from meanness, and few things could please him more than tripping a smaller kid into kissing the pavement with splayed lips. It was so cheap in exertion, so productive in humiliation. But he was really his own gang. The meanest kids appreciated his hegemony and stuck to him like magnets on a refrigerator. In a way, I was their reason for being. I gave Willie something around which to organize.

Big Willie persisted in the belief that because I was a China Boy, I had to be special. And special people, like whites, had to have money, somewhere. For years I struggled with the sense that Big Willie and Edna were related to each other.

A dime taken from any other kid was a good deal. A dime from me would cause Willie to expect more.

"No have no mo'!" I cried, enraged that my words had no effect.

"Boool*shit!*" said his fists, with grand eloquence.

My yelps and tears did nothing to stop the whippings; the blows ended with the passing of the honor of the moment. As the months unrolled, the protocols changed, becoming briefer and more efficient. I had to relearn the system while making new book on the short little punchers who were coming up in the ranks, pounding their way up the order.

I knew that this was my fault. Bad karma. Some epic insult to Heaven. I wrestled with its etiology; what exactly had I done to make all this necessary?

I went to the attic, looking out the window on the right.

"I sorry!" I shouted in my mind. Okay, I bad boy say all things wrong with bad face and Mah-mee not come back! I understand! No more lessons!

Christian churches seemed to be of little benefit. I took control by becoming an informal Buddhist, drawing from the well of our unconscious past and Mother's pre-Christian ideals. I stopped stepping on ants, and, unlike other kids, did not throw rocks at birds in the park or skip stones at ducks at Stow Lake. I was infinitely kind to babies. I even said hello to Evil, the voracious bulldog.

"Don eat me, doggie *pungyoh,*" I said.

I went back to the attic to look into the sky. I saw little detail of anything in those days, so seeing God was as easy as perceiving anything else. I knew I had yelled at him earlier, and regretted it. But even when I had God's undivided attention, and was not motivated by frustration, and had mouthed songs in a score of his churches bearing different names and honoring different tribes, I doubted the benefit of devotion. I sat beneath the attic window, waiting for God to lay a soft-edged parallelogram of light on the bare wood floor, shifting to place my body within it. I used Songhai, God's language.

"I trying hard, God, like Han Tzu-ren the good student," I said, referring to the smart, fabled boy with the single birthday from *The Tales of Lu Hsun*. I spoke into the light from the pane. "I no hurt living things. I set table *hao dao,* right way, fork on left. I listen in your temple house, in all temple house you have. I like sing songs to you. I like Jones Syensheng, Lamport Syensheng, Hogan Syensheng, Lowry Syensheng, Cutler Syensheng, all temple teachers. McCready Syensheng, from St. Ignatius, too. You stop beatings. No more beating, please, please God. I do what you say. Promise, hope die."

I looked at the sunlight. I could see the tiny dust particles in front of my eyes. I perceived no sign, but could hear Edna stirring below. I blinked several times and held myself very still, so he would know that I was attentive and studious. Nothing happened. I took a deep breath and prepared for the street. God was busy with other people, probably firstborns.

I became adept at avoiding the first punches, but could never dodge all of them. When the first blow landed, I took to my feet. I ran with all the motivation my little psyche could gather. But flight was uncool, and it galvanized the other kids to a packlike response, my speed a spur to their own efforts. I was as fast as any kid on the block, but I ran stupidly, unable to plan moves because everything in front of my eyes was a generalized blur while everything in my brain had evacuated to my lower intestines.

They chased, blocked, and channeled me into a fence or a wall, there to perform the honor of single combat with the one I had fled, serving sentence for violating every rule on the street. The crying confused them, for it was the culmination of too many street taboos in a single child.

"China Boy, you'se a chinkface clown, a *joker*," said Tyrone. "You'se a gimp. You'se stupid as jasper. Can talk none. An you'se deaf, too. Can fight. An man, den you *cry?*"

Younger kids coming up in the ranks could learn how to hit another kid in the face—a rite of passage from arm and stomach punches—by practicing on me. I served a purpose in the community, the way hydrants do for dogs.

"Ming-li," I said. "Boys fight in China?"

"Boys!" she said. The sisters had been born with good looks and had always drawn boys' attention. She was now at an age when she began to suspect the reason, and she didn't like it. "I don't remember too much about China. But I think they fight everywhere!"

"I don't like fight. Don't think Mother want me to fight. She say bad for karma. What you think?" I asked.

"I think it's worse for your face," she said softly.

9

TOUSSAINT

A rail-thin nine-year-old named Toussaint LaRue looked on during these beatings and only hit me once. I therefore assumed that he occupied some lower social niche than mine. Like a snail's.

He took no pleasure in the China Boy rituals. He instead talked to me. I suspected that he had devised a new method of pain infliction.

"Toussaint," he said, offering his hand. "Ya'lls supposed ta shake it." He grinned when I put my hand out with the same enthusiasm with which I would pet Mr. Carter's bulldog. Toussaint, like Evil, had a big gap between his front teeth.

Toussaint would become my guide to American boyhood.

My primary bond to him was for the things he did not do. He did not pound or trap me. He never cut me down. Or laughed with knives in his eyes. Then he opened his heart by explaining things to me, giving me his learning, and taking me into his home.

"China. Don be cryin no mo'. Don work on dis here block, no sir, Cap'n! Give 'er up. When ya'll cry, hol' it insida yo'self. Shif ' yo' feet an air-out, go parkside. Preten ya'll gone fishin. Don run, now. Ain't cool.''

"Fish in park?'' I asked.

"Cheez! Ya'll don colly nothin! Ferget da fish, China. Dry yo' tears.''

He told me about the theory of fights. That kids did it because it was how you became a man later on.

"Momma tole me,'' he said, "in ole days, no Negro man kin hit or fight. We belongs to da whites, like hosses.

"Man fight 'notha man, be damagin white man goods. So he get whipped. An I mean *whipped.*'' He shook his head and rubbed the top of it, easing the pain of the thought.

"Now, ain't no mo' dat,'' he said, smiling. "We kin fights, like men.'' He was speaking very seriously. Fighting was a measure of citizenship. Of civilization. I didn't think so.

"China, stan up.''

"Why?'' I whined.

"Putchur fists up. Make a fist! Right. Bof han's.

"Dis one—,'' he said, holding my left. "It fo' guardin yo' face. Dis here one—dat's fo' poundin da fool who call ya out. Here come a punch, and ya'll block it. China—you listenin ta me?''

"No fight, no reason!'' I said hotly.

"No reason!?'' he yelled. "You can fight wif no *reason*? Boy! Whatchu *talkin* about?''

Uh-oh, I thought. Toussaint's hands were on his hips.

"Evera kid on dis here block like ta knock you upside da head and make you *bleed* and ya'll got no *reason*? China. Ain't no dude in da Handle got mo' cause fo' fightin *evera* day den *you*!''

"Too many boy fight,'' I said, drawing back from his heat.

"Uh-*uh*! No sir, Cap'n! Big-time nossir! Lissen. Some kids, dey fight *hard*. But ain't *never* gonna be no gangin up on one kid. *Dat* ain't cool.'' He shook his head. "Kid stan on his feet. No one else feet. Ain't *nobody* gonna stan inaway a dat. An youse best colly dat."

"Hittin' long," I tried.

"Say what?" he said.

"Long. Not light!"

"Wrong? Ya'll sayin fightin's *wrong*?"

"Light," I said.

"Howzat?"

"Bad yuing chi," I explained.

"Say *what*?"

"Bad, uh, karma!" I said, finding the East Indian word often used by my sisters.

"Well, China, ya'll thinks awful funny. Don have nothin ta do wif no *caramels*. No matta Big Willie take yo' candies. Ain't *candies*. It not bein *chicken*. Not bein yella. Ya'll don havta like it. Sakes, China, no one like ta Fist City. Well, maybe Big Willie, he like it. But like it or don like it, no matter none. Ya'll jus *do* it."

He invited me to play in his house. Many of the games involved capturing cockroaches. "Ya'll ready?" he would ask, and I would nod, nervously. Toos would kick the wall next to the sink, and roaches would slither out of the dust and the cracked plaster. Toos would use his plastic cup, smacking it quickly onto the floor, smiling as he watched the captured roach's antennae struggle to escape, its hard body clicking angrily against the plastic.

He made his closest buddies tolerate me. His mother took me to the church of Reverend Jones on Sundays until Edna changed my religion. The simple presence of his company, and that of his pals, saved me from innumerable trashings and gave me time to breathe.

I had never had a friend before, and I cared for him as few lads have for another. My heart fills now when I think of him. That will never change.

Toussaint was, next to me, the skinniest kid on the block. He ran no faster than I since he lacked the sin-

cerity of my efforts, but he was as tough as a slum rat
and had the guts of Carmen Basilio. Basilio, the big-
headed middleweight who fought while his blood ran
down his bruised face like cascading crimson rain in
a summer monsoon. Basilio, whose busted face was
on the front page of every pinned-up sports section in
every barbershop in the city. Kids respected bravery
above all else. It was what allowed you to put your
pants on in the morning.

My courage was so low that putting on my big-boy
underpants was a task. Toussaint was deemed crazy to
buddy with me. But he was my friend because I needed
one. He got nothing for himself, in the hard world of
our peers' respect, for his generosity.

Outside of a table service, we had few possessions
and less cash, but Toos's home made ours look like a
gilded palace of Babylon. The LaRue family lived in
a windowless converted storage room in a shambling
tenement on Masonic, next door to Brook's Mortuary.
The stone steps to the main door were chipped, crumbling, and dangerous for old people and toddlers. The
entryway was a garbage dump for rotted food, and the
stairways reeked of old and pungent uric acid.

A sad, small alcoholic named Sippy Suds lived next
door to Toussaint. Suds's apartment produced the worst
smell in the Panhandle, a rancid sour waft of vomit
and urine so strong in the closed space of the hallway
that it made you crazy with the badness of it. He used
to mess on himself. Suds was one of several people in
the 'hood whose speech evaded understanding. I
thought it was related to my eyes. Whenever I concentrated and tried to fight through his thick, inebriated
Mississippi babble, my eyes watered from the pungent
toxins in the air. Suds had everything no one wanted,
down to flies that liked his clothes and odors that would
cause others to change jobs.

Many of the kids on the block despised Suds, taking
his pitiful coins by incessant begging.

"C'mon, Suds, gimme nickel. Yeah! Gimme dollah!"

Toussaint respected him.

"Leave da man be," he said to a whole battalion of yammering kids. "Ain't cool, takin poor man's coins. C'mon! Back off!" he shouted, pushing them back. " 'Sides. Man yoosta be a fighta," he said.

Heck, I thought. *Everyone* around here is a fighter.

I had seen dead rats before in our house, looking pitiful and scary in the traps, their little feet tucked up in death, thick round tails looking like remnants of ancient lizards. But I had never seen families of them alive. They were on Toussaint's stairs, sluggish, bunched up, and squeaky, and the first time I saw them I stopped and cried. Toussaint looked at me, nodding his head. The rats were pushy and one ran over my foot, small, heavy, sharp-clawed, and warm.

"Won hurtcha none," he said, taking my arm as I began to faint.

An elderly and toothless woman lived in a shamble of newspapers and produce cartons on top of the stairs in the hall. Toussaint called her Missus Hall. She wore old shawls, discarded and unmatched men's shoes, and staggered on broken hips with wriggling loose shoelaces, aided by a short stick wrested from a fruit crate. She would sit on the neighborhood stoops, her crackled fingers pulling splinters from each other, her aged and wrinkled face scrunched with the effort of finding the torment in her hands. During these efforts, her fleshy nose could touch her lips. She was missing clumps of hair, eyelashes, eyebrows. Missus Hall did not look like someone who had been very pretty in her youth. But her durability, her will to survive, were attractive, and I liked her very much.

My mother had been beautiful. And she had died.

Missus Hall would relieve herself on old newspapers in the alleyways on Central Avenue. She never spoke to anyone but would nod at Toussaint, who brought her shares of their meager food. The LaRue and the

Ting families did not look even a little bit alike, but we had the same caloric intake, while enjoying strong differences on the meaning of Christian charity.

Mrs. LaRue offered to feed me as well, and I was inclined to eat anything that wasn't going to run away from me. This easily included plain, unbuttered grits, which resembled *tze*, rice gruel. But Toussaint's friends never took food from his mother. Her son was too thin.

One Halloween night, after I had been friends with the LaRues for more than five years, Missus Hall smiled at me. I remember that when she showed her teeth I thought she was angry. It took a moment to realize that she was greeting me with a smile, and I beamed back at her, offering her witches' teeth candy, the world full of light.

I asked Mrs. LaRue why Missus Hall never spoke.

"I honestly don't know, Kai," she said. "I figure somethin almighty drastic happened in her life, and it probly happened twice. Once early, and once late. She's not gonna do nothin fancy with her life. She's jes getting ready for the next blow."

The LaRue home had no furniture, only milk cartons and fruit crates that his momma got from the Reliance Market.

Toussaint had no toys and never asked to play with those belonging to others. He had no father. His mother was wonderful and caring and had convinced Toos that toys and living fathers were not necessary in this mysterious physical world. She carried the whole load, all the way. Toussaint had the gift of love, and they shared everything they had. I was testament to that fact. His smile, shining from a high-cheekboned, high-foreheaded, almost skull-like face, was beatific and had the force of the Prophet. I thought he was the handsomest boy in the world.

As a streetfighter, Toussaint was unusual. He cared nothing for style, which was becoming an extremely big deal to the others.

"Toos," said Jerome Washington. "Ya'll fights like a ole' lady. Ya'll fights like Missus Hall." He giggled. "Ain't dat right, Toos?" Jerome was not looking for a fight. He just enjoyed stirring feces with his tongue.

"Dat probly be true, Jerome," said Toussaint, slowly. He was smiling, frustrating Jerome in some mysterious way. Jerome cursed and moved on.

"See, China? Jerome don mess wif me. He wanna hurt mah feelins, an I jes talk blahdee-blah trash back at 'em. 'China Bashers.' Dat's a lota *crap*. Misser Pueblo, in Cutty's Garage. He tole me: fight fo' da fight. Don pay no mind ta no lookers. Style, dat fo' *girls*.

"Fists. Be fo' da boy dookin Fist City wif ya."

Toos threw unending series of berserk punches, ignoring incoming rounds as if they were raindrops on a pleasant spring day. He would punch until the fight was over—until Toussaint collapsed or the other kid stopped. I didn't know how he could do that.

When he fought, the smile beat feet, and he became all business. He did not have to do this often. It usually occurred when a Haight kid crossed the border of Fell Street and strutted north up Masonic, looking to break some bones.

Toos's home was on the cross-'hoods thoroughfare. It was Indian Country; trouble came calling with the rising sun.

Toos was skinny and occasionally got picked. He would stand up straight, like an older boy, and roll his shoulders back, like a grown man. He would measure the challenge, giving the Handle crosser a chance to move on. Sometimes his quiet, unfearing gaze was as articulate as my mother's face. When parley failed, he met aggression with his own fury. He was never called out twice by the same youth.

The Haight, six blocks south, was bogeymanland. Boys carried knives, men had zip guns, and women looked more dangerous than twenty San Juan street-fighters with switchblades. Some of the Haight boys wore old-skinned Big Ben coveralls and carried barber shaving razors in the cup of the hand, hiding the flash of steel inside their arm-swaying struts. They could punch a guy and move on. It took a moment to realize that the face had been opened, blood everywhere, the searing pain following long moments after the incision.

"Ya'll stay outa dere," said Toussaint, pointing with a long and skinny thumb at our rival 'hood. "Be boogeymen, big-time."

Until I learned English, I understood it as The Hate. The Panhandle lay between our 'hoods like no-man's-land, a DMZ that operated without U.N. intervention. Panhandle boys entered the park with great care and only in daylight. It was a jungle of thick eucalyptus, corpses, tangled azalea, and memories of aimless nocturnal screams. Men gathered there at night to smoke and drink and discuss this new land of California. When they disagreed, people died.

The Haight was largely populated by trekkers from Alabama and Louisiana. Mrs. LaRue said their heartaches came from not having a minister. Reverend M. Stamina Jones had followed the LaRues, the Joneses, the Scotts, and the Williamses—the Panhandle families—from Georgia. Others in the neighborhood hailed from Mississippi, Maryland, and Tennessee. I thought they were names of streets.

"No ministers in the Haight, just knife fighters," she said. "They'se lost. Toussaint LaRue and Kai Ting, you listen to Momma! Don't be goin into the Haight, no how and no way. Now. *That* be gospel."

Toussaint taught me about music. He tried to translate the words of the chorus in the church of Reverend Jones, but I always suspected that he lacked certainty in his explanations. But he knew that the chorus moved me, and would rub the hair on my head whenever I found myself weeping in time with its singing. I did not have to be an Imperial Scholar to know that crying in this temple house was accepted; the congregation's choral majesty was salted with tears and accented by open weeping. Sobs often served as confirmation of the truth of Reverend Jones's ministry. A dry-eyed assembly meant that his delivery was off the mark.

Toos also introduced me to Mr. Carter, who owned Evil the bulldog. Mr. Carter was a shipyard worker at Hunters Point who lived across the street from us, with the LaRue home around the corner. He had a platoon of exwives, no prospects of any more, two radios and a record player, and everyone on the block liked him while hating his dog.

Evil was moody. Somedays he raised his black-and-white head to you on a loose leash, anxious for a pat, his eyes half-closed, his teeth looking sadly overused and brownishly old.

Other days he growled, the fangs angry and huge and brightly wet. He would run around like a broken top with his jaws open, all the kids screaming as they scattered. Evil never caught me; I was the flight expert. He would clamp his maws around a kid's leg and throw his neck back and forth and Mr. Carter would blow that whistle in Evil's ear until he let go. He would then use a fat clothes-hanger dowel to beat the starch out of the dog, and I was the only one who felt sorry for him.

"Oughta jes give dat dog *away*," said Toos.

I shook my head. "Give doggie mo' food," I said. "He too much hungry."

"China, you'se a very funny boy," he said. "Now. Don let no dog smell yo' fear. He smell dat, he get feared hisself and eat yo' pants in a *big* hurry."

The men who had been in the army would sit on the wide stairs of Mr. Carter's place and sing "What the Best-Dressed Man in Harlem Is Wearing Tonight," "The Blues in the Night," and I could close my eyes and sway to their unearthly beautiful voices. They also sang songs they called Jodies. I knew them; my father used to chant them while he chopped vegetables in the kitchen when our mother was still alive.

"Yo' momma was dere when ya lef'"
"YO' RIGHT!"
"Jody was dere when ya lef'"
"YO' RIGHT!"
"Sound off—"
"ONE-TWO!"
"Sound off—"
"THREE-FO'!"
"Bring it on down—"
"ONE-TWO-THREE-FO'!"
"ONE-TWO-THREE-FO'!"

"Jody got somethin dat you ain't got"
"I'S BIN SO LONG AH ALMOS' FO'GOT"
"Yo' baby's as lonely as lonely can be"
"WIF ONLY JODY FO' COM-PANY"
"Ain't it great ta have a pal"
"TA HELP KEEP UP HER MO-RALE"
"Sound off. . . ."
"Yo' not gonna get out till da enda da war"
"IN NINET'IN HUNDRA' AN' SEVENTY-
  FOUR. . . ."

Adults and kids gathered on Mr. Carter's stoop to sing and clap hands, or to gently swing to "Harlem Nocturne" and the high throaty jazz of Billie Holiday's "Strange Fruit," "The Way You Look Tonight," and "God Bless the Child." Toos told me that the words to that song meant that if God did not love you, you were soon dead, because little came to short people without God's grace.

"Good news is, China," said Toos, "dat God love all chilun."

"Me, too?" I asked.

"Dat *gotta* be true," he said. "God get dibs on all da little chilun he kin find. And," he said, elbowing me, "you'se little."

We would keep time and tap with one foot while keeping the other ready to exit stage left if Evil felt the urge. The muse didn't come cheap in the Panhandle.

"Mista Carter," said Toussaint's mom. "That's not right, namin a dog Evil. You can come up with a better name'n that, I know you can. Callin somethin a name sometime make it so."

"Charlotte, you think it be a big favor to all de chilun on dis block be comin up ta dis here dog an callin 'em *Spot*? or *Fido*?

"See. His firs' name, it was Winston. The name offered no warnin. Folks like ta pet 'em. Den he start ta eat kids? He gots too much crust. I call 'em what he is: Evil." He whacked his pants leg with the dowel.

Kids learned to make their own music, without radios. I thought this was because of Evil, since the price of listening to radios could be a pint of dog-drawn blood. But I was wrong. Kids, even poor and unhappy ones, love to sing, warbling the purity of expression, the unsullied and miraculous poetry of a child's honesty. Happy kids sing better. Toos sat on his crumbling steps with Titus McGovern and Alvin Sharpes—boys who had pledged their lives to him—to sing the "Papa Ditty," and other rapadiddle tunes from the not-so-distant South.

> *"Well, I don know but I been tole,*
> *Papa gonna buy me a pile a coal.*
> *If dat coal don burn fo' me,*
> *Papa gonna take me to da sea.*
> *If dat sea don make me wet,*
> *Papa gonna sink us deeper in debt.*
> *If dat debt don eat our food,*
> *Papa gonna thank da good Saint Jude."*

And so on.

Each kid would sing a two-line stanza, making it up as he went. I always shook my head, lowering it as I blushed when it was my turn.

"Dang!" cried Alvin Sharpes. "Lookit China's

face. It all red! How you do dat, China?'' It was easy.
I couldn't rhyme.

"Missa LaRue," I asked, struggling to align the *L*'s
and the *R*'s. "Kin rearn me 'Papa Ditty'?''

"The 'Papa Ditty'? I don't think I know that, Kai.
Can you sing a little of it for me?''

I tried. She laughed and hugged me.

"Oh, sweetnin, that's 'The Mockinbird's Song.'
Listen to me," she said, bending over, her smoothly
angular and pretty face bright with life, looking at me
with a great smile, singing in a deep mystic voice that
scratched the itches in my heart.

> *"Well, I'll tell you what I've learned:*
> *Papa's gonna buy me a mockinbird.*
> *If that mockinbird don't sing,*
> *Papa's gonna buy me a diamond ring.*
> *If that diamond ring don't shine,*
> *Papa's gonna buy me a bottle of wine.*
> *If that bottle of wine don't pour,*
> *Papa's gonna take us to the shore. . . ."*

"My momma rike shore, rike ocean," I said.

"Well, Kai, that big blue sea, it's somethin, all
right."

Toussaint told me that Big Willie Mack, the glandular
error in the guise of a twelve-year-old, had been the
first to punch me on my inaugural day on the street.
Big Willie was the toughest dude on the block, a bad
combination of vicious clothes-taking bully and mean,
gutsy fighter.

Toussaint had hit me on the arm that day with that
second, harmless blow, to make sure that Willie didn't
wind up and do it again.

"China, ya'lls gotta fight. Pretty soon, he be takin
yo' clothes."

"No. Crows too small. Him long size," I said.

"China. He don't take 'em ta wear. He take 'em to *take 'em*. You'se gotta punch it out wif him, China."

"Ohnry make worse, mo' hit."

"Den *you* hit back mo'. Dat how it is. It hard be livin, be a stan-up-boy on dis here block, ya'll don fight. Don havta *win,* jes *fight.* Make it so's da other boy think fightin you's too much work! Make it easy on *bof* of us."

"Kin *you* whup Big Wirry?" I asked.

"Nah, don think so. But he know I fights 'em, won give in. He wan *my* shoes, he gonna havta give me some *blood.* "

We both looked at Toos's shoes. I didn't think Toos had to worry about anyone taking them unless Evil went crazy or a starving rat was driven to extreme means.

I tried to explain yuing chi, the responsibility of the future, God's ever-watchful scorecard, to Toussaint, but the concept exceeded my vocabulary. I had understood the idea so easily when it was conveyed by the dark, shimmering, expressive eyes of my mother. I was so anxious to explain that fighting was wrong, and would cause later pain, but winning this inarticulate debate was as difficult as prevailing in its subject matter.

I thought desperately about fighting but could not figure it out. I would be noticed, cut down, called horrific names, shoulder-bumped or shoved into the soft tar of the old streets of the Handle. A kid would challenge me and fear would rise inside my stomach like fog on the Bay and swamp me. My lights would get punched out and I would bawl like a newborn.

Flight always overcame Fight.

The very best I could do was control my tears, to a point. It was my only victory over the weakness of my body, the paucity of my combat power, the horror of fighting.

"China, I need yo' help someday too," said Toos.

I looked at him, confused.

"Say dude from da Haight strut here wif a razor, break mah bones and bleed me. Hustle to yo' door, ya'll lemme in. Right?''

I thought of Edna. Edna wouldn't let *me* in.

"Hmm," I said.

Toussaint was a preacher of the handshake. He already knew at this tender age that people got by because they gave each other the biggest gift in the book: time. His momma provided it for him whenever he wanted it. They had a handshake on it, and it gave him the strength of angels.

"You'all lookin at me kinda strange, Kai. Whatcha thinkin?'' said his momma, as Toos went out the door.

"Toos ask fo' wata. You *give* wata.''

She studied me for a bit, passing me a sad little cup of water, as well. I drank. "Say that again?'' she said. So I did.

"Kai. I love my son. Now look here. *Everybody* love their kids. Yo' daddy and his wife, they surely love you, too. Jus' everabody don't know *how.*

"If the Good Lord took my boy from me I would curl up and die; I truly would,'' she said very solemnly. "He sent me Toussaint LaRue so's I could *love* him, give him my life, my heart.'' She smiled. "I have the Lord Jesus and I have Toussaint, and they'se my joys.

"Kai. You 'member this, chile. Someday you'all gonna have yo' own little Kai, a little Janie Ting. When yo' child want yo' time, you *give* it. That's our—our *callin.* I *love* my boy, but sometime he want ta play the cockroach game and I'm jes sick of it? Oh, Lord, *really sick of it.*'' She looked down at the old floor, clicking her tongue. "Or, he tell me the mos' *borin,* stop-your-mind stuff *ever*? My little man, Toussaint, he tell the longest and mos' unfunniest jokes in the world! But I *listen,* and I laugh fo' his joy, and I play him roaches, cuz I'm his momma, and he's my son. It's my God-given duty.''

She dried her hands on a rag, and exhaled, looking

away from me. "Toussaint's daddy got killed in truck acciden' in Benning," she said softly. "He was an officer. He went inta the army a private, and came back a cap'n, two bright silver railroad tracks on his collar. Lord, what a man he was! Well. The war, it was over, and he made it back from overseas, a pure hero, and he gave me Toussaint, and then we lost him. . . ." Her voice faded.

"He was a good man, Little Kai, and I miss him *evera day.*" Her voice was choked. She stopped to blow her nose, shaking her head, hot tears coursing down her cheeks. "God wanted him bad, and took him." She looked toward the door. "Oh, Lord. What a price You exact. . . .

"John LaRue made a promise to me. I think his son done made one to you. Promises be powerful things. I take care of my son's wants. Then he give water to other men when they need it. And we'll have another John LaRue in the world. You want some more water?"

That was yuing chi, karma! And she let Missus Hall and the rats live on the stairs, and roaches in the wall. Mrs. LaRue was Chinese! She just didn't *look* it.

Could you give water to children who asked for it *and* beat the stuffing out of them if a fight was offered? I frowned with the difficulty of the riddle. She was offering me more water.

I took the plastic cup from Mrs. LaRue again, looking at the liquid within it as I drew it to my mouth. The plastic was old and scarred, with a history probably longer than mine. Innumerable scratches and half-cracks made it look tired, as if the serving of its masters and the catching of roaches had somehow cost too much. The water inside the cup sloshed, like the surf in the ocean, and for a transcendent moment all the scale and sense of proportion in the world dissolved, and I could see my mother placing her feet in the roaring waters of the cup. She was communicating with Na-Gung, an ocean away, and with me, from another world.

My eardrums tickled, making me shudder, with her reaching for me. The cup was against my lip, and I stared inside it, cross-eyed. I could not drink this water.

"Tank you. Momma," I said. "I keep wata?"

"You want ta take it on home?" she asked.

"No. Want keep here, on sink. Same wata," I said. "Special. Uh, big-time, special."

"You can take it, chile."

"No," I said, shaking my head. "Mo' betta here." I heard Toos come in. Mrs. LaRue took the cup and placed it on the sink.

"China. Ya'll wanna be mah fren'?" asked Toos. Mrs. LaRue smiled and moved away from my field of vision. Maybe three feet.

"Chure, yep," I said. I sensed something weighing in the balance, an unasked question, a favor awaiting fulfillment.

"Den shake on it," he said, extending his hand. Again? I wondered. He took my hand and molded it into his. His was so hard, so rough.

"Squeeze, squeeze hard, China," he said, "like milk'd come out if ya squoze hard. You'se gotta know how." I gripped, and he smiled.

"Now. We'se frens, fo' sure," he said.

"An you can ask him yo' question, honey," said Momma.

"China," said Toos.

"Toos?" I said.

"China. Tell me 'bout yo' daddy."

I frowned. "Tell what?" I asked.

"Anythin, China. Jes *talk* 'bout him."

I began breathing heavily, not knowing what to say.

"I think yo' daddy was in the war, right?" said Mrs. LaRue. I nodded. "He in China army, for war," I said. "He fry airprane wif guns, bomb. He—" I made motions with my hands—"fall in pallashoot. Shoot gun. Save my ma-ma." I was licking my lips. "He very smart. Read books. Pray catch wif me. . . ."

There was a long silence.

"Thanks, chile," said Momma. "Listen. You share yo' daddy with Toussaint, here? Dat's what frens do."

Toussaint was all smiles, and I halfway grinned at him, trying to hide my teeth so the Teeth God would not want them.

It was now another day, and my friend, my friend of the handshake, my friend of the water, was staring at me. I jumped a little when I realized he had been staring at me.

"China, ya'll knows how ta laff?" asked Toos. We had been playing marbles. I was pretty good at marbles, for the short shots. I was also becoming something of a demon in penny-pitching, and card-tossing. Parlor games, not at the level of the Bigs of street-thumping and ball-playing, but something, after all. It was all in the wrist.

"Chure, yep," I said, worried by his question.

He opened his eyes wide and showed his teeth. He giggled. It was high, and silly, and warm.

"So les hear yo' laff!" he giggled.

I started to explain to him about the Teeth God, realizing that I could neither describe it nor prove its existence. I didn't even know if it was a boy or a girl. This was, like karma, a matter of faith. I suddenly wondered what all this god-fearing was worth. Mother had respected every god known, and they had taken her.

I opened my mouth and tried to make a laughing sound. It must've been ridiculous, because Toos bent over and guffawed, slapping his knees and putting his head between his knees while making a wonderful sound of a strange animal. My ears perked as I heard what I could later favorably compare to a spasm-ridden rum-crazed jackass. Now I was hearing something that reminded me of the distant laughter of my father. I giggled with him, still holding back.

Even through the laughter came the whistle of my stepmother. She never called when I needed her.

I could not discuss my street whippings at home. Stepmother Edna pretended that no problem existed, washing out the blood from my clothes with astounding tolerance. I began to believe that she took pleasure in my fear. I felt that my shame was mine, and somehow my father's and even my mother's, and did not see it as transferable.

Janie was involved in a struggle for survival with Edna. It was a war between two de facto mother figures. One by blood and death, one by marriage and expectation, neither by choice.

As the lastborn kid of four, I did not understand Janie's tenacious resistance to Edna's supreme power. Kids in the lower birth order, like me, seldom resisted parental authority as did the firstborn, the vanguards. Jennifer Sung-ah and Megan Wai-la were in Berkeley; Janie was now the functional older sibling.

Edna was a grown-up and could slap you silly and dance fandangos on your face. But she hadn't touched Jane for months. If Edna had left me alone like that I would have written poetry for her.

"Kai. I'm doing this for both of us. She is *not* our mom."

"I know dat," I said. I just didn't know what it meant. Janie's eyes were bright in anger.

"Edna told me not to read this to you," she said, pulling a stained and torn book from her aging schoolbag. "It's called *Hansel and Gretel*. It's about a stepmother who gets the father to get rid of the kids. Edna threw it out, and I dug it out of the garbage." Janie looked very intense, very determined.

We sat on the front stairs of our house. I pretended to look at the book, but was watching for Big Willie and the Bashers.

"You China Boy sister?" asked Reginald Tufts.

"His name is Kai," said Janie. "Can you say that? Kai."

"Kai," said Reginald. My mouth was, again, as open as the Red Sea was for Moses. Hearing a boy say my first name was astonishing, and I squinted with the pressure of it, waiting to see what else in the world might change next.

"I'm going to read a book. Want to listen?" she asked.

"A book? Yeah!" he cried, and I glared at him, not wanting to share Janie with a Basher, or a friend of a Basher. Even if he had said my name.

Janie opened the book, which was missing its cover.

"Once upon a time," she began, "there was a poor woodcutter who lived at the edge of a large forest with his wife and two children. The boy was named Hansel, and the girl was named Gretel. Many years before, his wife had died, and he had remarried. They had always been poor. . . ."

Toos and Alvin Sharpes arrived and sat on the stairs to listen to the story and stare at the storyteller. Janie smiled at them and received their smiles in return. I grinned.

The stepmother in this story gave the two children a last meal and left them in the woods to be taken by wolves. She had done this to allow the father and stepmother to live without the burden of the kids, whose voracious appetites were consuming too much of the limited food. It was a credible tale.

I later asked Toos what he would do if his momma left and another mother moved in.

"My momma, she no go nowhere wif out me. Dere ain't no other momma," he said.

"But she go bye-bye anyway," I said.

"Den I goes wif her."

"If she jus, *gone?*"

"I fin her," he said.

"Can fin her, den. . . ?"

"Keep lookin," he said.

"Where rook?" I asked.

"Dunno, China. Lord. *All* over." He looked at me.

"Ya'll miss yo' momma, doncha. Yeah." Then he looked up, squinting. "I 'member her. She yoosta tote da um-brella when dere was no rain. Ya'll was a big saprise, comin outa dat 'partment. Didn know you'se in dere."

I looked down at the stairs.

"Ya'll don like yo' stepmomma?"

I shook my head, fearing that somehow, even around the corner of buildings and the rise of streets, she knew I was admitting it, and that this knowledge would hurt me.

"She be a white lady," he said, and I nodded. "Wif yella hair," he added. "Don think she like *us*," he concluded.

"What I do, Toos?" I asked.

"She yo momma, now. Dang, China. I get it; dat's hard." He studied it for a bit. "I'd as' da Lord."

"I did dat," I said.

To my father, the combat between the females was Women's War, the incomprehensible tensions between disenfranchised females. In Shanghai, there was an unquestionable hierarchy, an immutable order of rank. It did not call for the involvement of men, and he had no experience to make himself Ward Cleaver, who in any event was a fantasy designed to sell Mapo. He could not find an intellectual guide to the current problem and knew that he did not wish to reestablish the old order. I found guidance in comic books.

I loved Superman and Mighty Mouse. I had lost my funnies in the revolutionary storm. Alvin Sharpes had a deep and endless collection and I began to draw from his castaways. I read them, two inches from my face, again and again. I began to imagine myself as a fighter. Who did good for others and beat the crap out of bad guys. Good karma. I projected myself into the cartoon sequences. I was unconquerable. Here I come, to save the day. . . . It means that Mighty Mouse is on his way. . . .

After my stunning victories over evil incarnate, I received the appreciative accolades of my family, laurels from a grateful nation, a citation from the President of the United States, free milk at our doorstep, and a new copy of *The Tales of Lu Hsun*.

After a pounding on the street, I would take out my comics and pore over them with shaking hands and a teary face, trying desperately to incorporate their messages into my body. But the correspondence-school method of streetfighting proved unsuccessful.

Then I tried reason. Be pal? I would offer. Pow! I don wan twubble wit you. Wham! Here, candy? Snatch!

Forget reason. I returned to comics and running.

Then Edna rediscovered the comic books, and they were gone.

I wondered if I was going crazy. I would awaken at night, crying from a dream in which I was fleeing my stepmother. Edna would enter my room and slap me in an effort to stop the weeping, which had awakened her. By the time I figured out that the dream had merged with reality, she was gone and I would squint at the closed door, trying to separate images of light and dark.

Despite the fact that I now had Toussaint and his mother in the periphery of my life, I tried to run away again.

Knowing that silence was imperative to successful flight, I took my time. It was not difficult to sneak down the staircase, my footfalls absorbed by the carpet that had through long wear become part of the risers. The front door made a sound like a cherry bomb when opened by the remote handle. I had seen Father lubricate it. I put oil in the hinges and gave the task five minutes, and the door opened with all the sound that a mouse makes when it sniffs cheese.

Golden Gate Avenue was utterly dark and surprisingly cold, the lone streetlamp at the corner of Central Avenue offering few clues and no warmth. But the street was mine, surrendered only for blinding moments as cars with overbright headlights passed.

The first time a car approached I ran from it, thinking it was an agent of Edna in hot pursuit. I could run very fast on a cold night on an empty sidewalk, my lungs bellowing as I humped arms high and hard to let my legs pump, my head vibrating synchronously with the effort as I fled my fears.

I roamed McAllister, leaning against the cold steel doors of Cutty's Garage, peering into the barred windows of the Reliance Market, missing the winos who kept guard at the Double Olive Bar, trying to recapture the now departed aromas of sizzling french fries in the General Lew Wallace Eatery. I wondered if Rupert and Dozer, the fratricidal siblings, argued after they closed the Eatery and went home to the large apartment building on Grove. Without the aromas of food, McAllister smelled sour and old. I played imaginary checkers on the linoleum grid of the barbershop floor. I projected the more complex figures of Chinese chess, *shiang chi,* onto the black-and-white squares, but could not remember all the moves for both players.

I strolled to Broderick Street, over the pavement where I had once raced when I had a home in which to hide. I looked through the iron-grate fence of Fremont Elementary, retracing beatings by Big Willie and the Bashers. I surveyed the kickball-field benches, the lunch tables, where food had been taken and little bodies stomped. I looked at that spot of the yard, knowing a truth lay in it. I looked away.

Cats chased shadowy rats on the street where Big Willie had stood on my chest. Dogs rousted garbage cans. One growled at me and I froze, waiting ten or fifteen minutes like a man who has stepped on a pressure-release-trigger landmine, until the dog had taken his pleasure with the waste. With light feet, his mangy tail down, he padded away from me and I breathed again.

This was my street, McAllister. Now, in the solace

of the night, with its bullies and angry words and fists
absent, I liked it. I wanted to sleep by day and to walk
McAllister to the east at night. It felt safe, the biting
cold welcome and fitting. For an instant, I did not
want to go any farther, my feet immobilized by the
vast, dark unknowns that surrounded the 'hood. I
wondered if *wupo*, witches, awaited me in side alleys,
or if *dufei*, bandits, were hoping to snatch the only
son of the Ting clan tonight.

Ah, I thought. The *wupo* is *inside* the house, not
here.

Feeling mildly suicidal, I crossed McAllister to Fulton, which was bold for any kid north of the park. I
headed south, keeping to the shadows, crossing Grove,
Hayes, and Fell, the final boundary between sanity
and simple stupidity. I watched the night traffic on
Fell, a big, wide thoroughfare. Where were these people going? Could I go too?

Now I was in the tall eucalyptus trees of the Panhandle itself, the glare of the streetlights swallowed in
the darkness of gnarled, interwoven trees. I was in the
demilitarized zone, the place of mysterious human
sounds, secret passions, and dark bleeding. This was
not a child's place.

I crept through the brush as only a boy with bad
night vision can. Slowly, patiently, silently, over a de-
tritus of cans, wrappers, boxes, papers. If I made a
noise, I stopped. I crawled past a man and a woman,
whispering to each other with an intensity beyond
comprehension. I shimmied up to a group of talkers
sitting around a burning trash can. The fire crackled
and cloaked my advance.

I listened to the men in the park. "Boogeymen"
from the Haight, with deep, gravelly, bitter voices,
raspy with old rumbling hungers. The humor was
strained. Some of the speakers were drunk and flared
at each other like the trash fire finding fuel to combust
in gunfirelike consumption.

What would they do if they found me? I wondered.

Nothing, I decided. They didn't care about little boys. There was little talk about sports and fighting. Someone mentioned Joe Louis, and I heard DiMaggio's name.

They were mostly concerned with women, and their meanness and beauty. The mystery of women. These men blamed women for all their woes. Always taking things, wanting more, refusing love, yelling, complaining, comparing. I nodded my head, watching the shadowed figures gesturing, belching in hunger, nodding heads, tippling bottles.

One man held their attention as he spoke of the great Southern Pacific trains that ran from the China Basin docks to Mexico with empty freight cars, no railroad police, and a free meal at the train stops for veterans. I was the son of a veteran. Did that count? I didn't have a mother. Did that matter?

China Basin. It was somewhere in San Francisco, and it sounded like China Boy, like me. It was *my* train. I could go to Mexico. No Edna. No Willie and no Bashers. I would be leaving Janie. Could I do that?

In my mind I heard the wail of the engine calling, its thunderous power promising fast, determined movement, high-pumping wheels chugging tirelessly, taking me away even while I slept in its cars.

I watched the firefly sparks of the trash fire flicker into the night sky, looking like the stack flames of a southbound freight, disappearing into the swallowing blackness. For years I would deride myself, assailing my manhood, for not taking the China Basin train. The decision had been in my hands, but I lacked the ability to seize an early opportunity to die a boy's lonesome death on a distant track.

When I reached Masonic and Golden Gate, I was drawn to Toussaint's apartment building. I climbed the outside stairs with great stealth, thinking of Mrs. LaRue, wanting a glass of water, happy with the mere thought that she was on the other side of the door, resting. Truly there, actually alive, to be seen and heard again. I touched a leg. A big leg. I knew that I was dead from fright and would be beaten afterward for clumsiness.

It was Sippy Suds, his horrendous odors mysteriously absent in the cool of the night. He stirred slightly and began to snore softly. He looked huge lying down, folded inside his faded, moth-eaten, navy pea jacket. In his bent, inebriated, staggering postures on the street, I had thought him as short as Missus Hall. He was actually a tall man. His hands were pinned between his drawn-up knees. They were huge, the fingers bent and black with the dirt of past labor. His wrists were bony but very thick. Hands that gave precious coins to greedy children.

His face looked as if it had been hit often by hard objects or by an angry stepmother. It was square and hard, different colors shading it. Bruising colors. His nose was very flat at the bridge, the bottom of the nose turned to the side, as if an anvil had been dropped on it from an angle. The closed, trusting eyes were surrounded by scars and small mounds of built-up skin. The rough pebbles of scar tissue interrupted the deep lines that laughter had once carved into his temples.

He was a fighta, Toussaint had said.

I sat next to him, looking at him, edging closer, absorbing his kindly silent companionship, feeling safety, defeating loneliness with every moment in his company. I held my breath.

Then we breathed together, and I matched his cycle, my small puff of air emerging with his thicker cloud, both of us slowly exhaling our fatigues with bright, streetlit, vaporous breath into the foggy night. My lungs filled with soulful strength.

I wanted him to awaken and to tell me about his fights. I wanted to hear that he had won, somehow, somewhere, in his past. Together, I thought, the two of us could do anything. I sat until my bottom ached from the hardness of the stairs, and I began shivering, my thin body capsized in cold.

Bye-bye Suds, I whispered, smiling as he stirred again. I returned with small steps to the house of my stepmother, ready for neither the beginning of sleep nor the start of day.

10

HECTOR PUEBLO

Salvation arrived near the middle of my first term on the street. It happened during my worst beating.

Little Aaron Williams was five and twice my size. Blessed with a roundness of body and limb, a breadth of chest and shoulders, he presented like a thoroughbred fighter, but fought like a dray horse. He had been scuffed a couple times in his first fights and had cried too loudly. His stock on the street was down, and he was itching for an opportunity to redeem it. That was my job.

As he looked at me, Aaron must have thought: Here come Chicken Little!

I cannot remember what stimulated the event, but I was in the middle of a routine panicked run and somehow, as I faced the motor traffic on the bad corner of Fulton and Masonic, Toussaint's urgings broke through, and I got tired of flight.

I felt my buddy's handshake, and I stopped. I stuck a fist in Little Aaron's face. I think the surprise of it exceeded the hurt, but he cried like a stuck pig while I shook my wounded hand, marveling at the fact that

I had somehow won. I had avoided a pounding. I should have said, Not so fast, hotdog. . . .

Anita Mae Williams was a tall and swift-limbed ten-year-old. She was beautiful, with a smile that tugged at the hearts of boys and a careful, watchful grace amplified by an elegant swan's neck that suggested unattainable royalty and wonderful, confusing, mesmerizing girlhood. She also had a sincere right cross. She was responsible for raising her baby brother Aaron. There were a lot of kids with that responsibility on the block. Janie was one of them, and these young girls shared in common the fact that they were serious about it.

When Anita Mae Williams found out that the China Boy had punched out her Little Aaron, she tracked me down. Later, when I discovered Western literature, I recognized in Inspector Javert the steadfast resolution of Anita Mae when she put me in her cross hairs.

I was on my return leg from Fremont, hustling down the clutter of McAllister, just past the drunks at the Double Olive Bar. I was stupidly smelling the fries at the door to the Eatery and wondering how angry Rupert the cook might be when she got me.

"Flies," I said, hesitantly. "Fl-ries. Uh, fl—"

Anita knocked me down and wasted me from the Reliance Market, on Lyon, all the way to Cutty's Garage on Central. She was stripping the skin from her knuckles, but all she could see was her baby brother's cut lip. I tried not to cry and then she hit me square in the nose. I hurt enough to scream, startling the winos and causing one of them to drop his paper-sacked Tokay on the street with a wet explosion of cheap glass and bad grapes. "Aww, shee-itt!" he complained.

This was a serious licking and it worsened when she tired of chasing me and picked me up, stuffing me into a square metal garbage can, the likes of which once adorned the streets of San Francisco. She began punching me methodically in the face, her grunts of effort so ugly, so unlike her delicate, angelic face.

I was hurt past crying, and I could sense in Anita's blows the momentary hesitation that all people feel when they are about to kill someone. She kept hitting my forehead, and penumbra replaced myopia, and my arms fell away, no longer offering interference.

A Mexican mechanic named Hector stopped it.

"Hey, girl," he said. "Park yo' fists! Boy don have no *sangre,* no blood lef fo' you. You made yo' point. You keep swingin, he gonna fo'get why you hate him. You bein a *pendeja,* chica."

Anita nodded, not knowing the foreign word but recognizing the truth. I knew it had stopped but the pain seemed to worsen. I tried to thank him but my lip was split, and a dislodged late baby tooth impeded articulate expression. I couldn't crawl out of the can. His rescue allowed me to sob and cry weakly, all I had left.

Hector extracted me from the steel box, which was like pulling a barbed fishhook, and took me into Cutty's rest room and cleaned me up, using fresh oil rags. The rags turned heavy with blood. My cheek was swollen like I had misplaced a tennis ball. My ears rang off and on like a broken telephone deep in my cranium and my lips began to swell toward Sutro Heights. Every now and again I sat down involuntarily. In the middle of all this I got the hiccups, and as he gave me a glass of water I tried to look for waves inside it, half cross-eyed. I began to laugh hysterically.

"Sorry I cly," I said to the world.

I felt safe in the garage. It smelled of dead grease. My blood was on his hands, on his T-shirt, and on his floor. He was not angry. Nor was Joe Cutty when he pulled out the engine from an old truck and walked over to inspect my body damage. I kept trying to wipe up the drops of blood on his concrete floor.

"Man, oh man," he said. "Don't sweat that. This

here's a garage, not an officers' club. That cheek could use a stitch. You gonna live, son?''

''Ah could sew that rip up,'' said a third man. It was Tom Molineaux, a small, wiry, jumpy sort of person who had just graduated from Polytechnic High. He called wrenches ''spanners'' and liked to spin them like batons. He was always eager to do what Joe called the ''shit details.'' He always was in a rush, working fast. He had received his draft notice for Korea.

''No, no,'' said Joe Cutty. ''That'd hurt more'n the tear.''

I was ready to move in.

''Hector. Who pounded this boy?'' asked Cutty.

''Anita Mae,'' he said. *''Hombre,* she was plenty P-O'd!'' There was a silence. A girl had just trashed a boy on McAllister. Wonders would never cease.

''Why she screw wif you so bad, chico?'' asked Hector.

''Hit bruddah,'' I squeaked.

''She hit her brother?'' asked Tom Molineaux.

I shook my head, and it hurt. I pointed at me. The men nodded. They knew that Anita Mae really watched out for Aaron.

''When yo' daddy come home, *niño*?'' asked Hector.

''Six,'' I said.

''Yo momma expec' you home now?''

I shrugged my shoulders and he nodded. Hector went into the office and came out with a stack of *Argosy* magazines and some Donald Duck comics. I smiled and he smiled.

I was reading about Huey, Louie, and Dewey's Woodchuck Guide and the Magic Flying Radish while Hector pulled chains, banged tools, hummed Navy tunes; Joe cranked ratchets; and Tom moved around the garage like a zephyr.

Then Anita Mae said, ''Hey, I'm sorry, China Boy. Doncha be hittin mah Little Aaron no mo'.''

I nearly jumped out of my socks. I was afraid of

talking to her. I nodded, my throat jammed, all the hurts in my head, mouth, and stomach coming back, with the hiccups. Her knuckles were skinned from tagging my face. I started to cry and she shook her head, her drop earrings bobbing, catching the fading light from the open garage doors. She walked off on her long legs.

Later, when I was twelve, and driven by blind ambition, and she was fifteen, and knew better, I asked her to marry me. She laughed in a deep rich woman's tone that made rejection both interesting and bearable.

Hector Pueblo was from Guadalajara, making him an outsider as well to the main culture of the Handle. He spoke blackgang Navy and black street with a Hispanic panache. He had been an unemployed carpenter until Joe Cutty hired him.

Cutty was huge, formed from a template that would have served two normal adults. He had a round face made jovial by bright, almost boyish eyes and eyebrows ridiculously small for a man his size. His biceps were as big as his head.

Joe Henry Cutty was like most of the men in the Panhandle. He had returned from the war, relieved to be alive and unsure about the future. With his savings, bolstered by intelligent poker play across the breadth of the Pacific, he managed to buy the garage from a redneck who viewed the black migration into California as the end of the free world. The seller had said to him, "Glad you're not like them other niggers. I can trust *you*."

Cutty smiled his slow smile that expressed no joy. He then lowered his offer to the owner by half, and the man took it, cursing himself and the black nation.

"Bastards trying ta get a good deal. Can you believe that shit?" the seller muttered to his god.

Cutty hired Hector after seeing his tattoos. Both of them had been Navy machinists. In Lingayen Gulf in 1944, their carrier groups had fought next to each other, and that had cemented it. Hector was heavily

muscled with long arms and big, high-knuckled hands
that caught sharp and hot metal surfaces and absorbed
grease. He and Joe Cutty were top mechanics, artisans
with wrenches, and they smelled like engines on a hot
summer day.

"*Joven,*" said Hector. "C'mon. We gonna hump dis
hill, go to your home." He pulled me out of the deep
couch, and kept his hand on my back as we trudged
up Central to my house.

"Lissen. Say *tío.* It mean 'uncle.' You unnerstan'?"

"*Tío,*" I said.

"*Joven.* You call me Tío Hector, hokay?"

I nodded. "Uncle" was *dababa.* Now I had two
uncles. He and Uncle Shim did not resemble each
other very much, and looking carefully at Hector while
we climbed the hill did not change the perception.

Edna did not want to let Hector or me in the house.
My father opened the door. He knew Hector and invited him in. Father and Edna looked at my face and
my clothing. Hector, wearing a nice Navy khaki shirt,
jumped right in.

"Missa Ting. Yo' boy, he need lesson in *boxeo,* in
pugilato, fists. I see him tussle, and ees *ugly.*" Hector
glanced at Edna, licking his lip nervously.

"He's *muy rápido,* you know, bery quick. Black boy
get in his face and firs' t'ree punches, firs' kick, yo'
boy go lik' dis an lik' dat, no touch." Hector twisted
his upper body, his arms up.

"But his eyes, dey get *muy grande* and he take to
feet an try to run home. Den dey take him down and
dey beat him."

He looked down at me and rubbed my hair with his
hand. He looked at me. I smiled, but only halfway;
Edna did not like Hector, his shirt, his speech, or the
hair-rubbing. Beatings were okay in our family, but
touching was taboo.

"Now wors ting, dis boy tink," pointing at me,
"ees cryin. Ain't bad, cryin." Hector could see that
Stepmother Edna was not buying it.

"*Los jóvenes,* de children, dey cry. Ees natural. You know, dey say, 'Cry Lika Baby'?" Hector smiled engagingly at Edna, a great, shining, teeth-gleaming, Cesar Romero, Gilbert Roland heart-warmer.

My father grinned. I smiled.

Edna's face said: No sale, you common laborer.

"Hokay. Not fightin, dot's bad news," Hector said forcefully and directly to my father, making my guts jump. I had a feeling our house confused him. He was not alone.

"Chinee boy gotta fisticuff, maybe mo' dan odder kids. He stand out, bery big-time. Yo'll better tell him dot, cuz cryin ain't de problem. *Boxeo, dot* de problem."

My father's face was impassive, but I felt grand relief. The reality of my life had come before him.

"Thank you," my father said, and I tried to keep my face passive, too.

Hector was trying to figure out Edna, whose stern disapproval was patent in the hallway. Hector's advice regarding the saving of my life did not belong in this house, either. His tattoos and muscled arms also felt out of place, and he put them behind him. I think he liked my father, because he said, "Missa Ting. I teach yo' boy *un poco.* But firs', you sen him to de Y.M.C.A. Dey teach him de basics, *las reglas.* De boy, he can come to Cutty's to learn. But, no way he come to hide." His arms were out, and I watched them, fascinated. He made a fist and cocked his right arm up, a gesture of strength and defiance.

"Den, I teach him *street,*" and he pumped it. His biceps bulged; the long muscles in his forearm popping. Edna glided out of the entryway and Hector ignored her. I breathed again.

The Y.M.C.A. cost twelve dollars every two months. At first, Stepmother Edna balked. But she realized that further beatings could result in medical bills. She had just discovered that we were not only poor, but very poor. She had restated her position that she did not want me in the house between school and dinner, or during sunlight on weekends. Six dollars a month. An investment in childcare.

Hector said good-bye. My father pointed to the old round leather hassock. I sat down and he turned on a table lamp. The hassock had once been green and red and was now a uniform brown. He cleared his throat. We had the best talk of my life to date.

"I was in Chinese Army," he said in a gruff voice, looking out the window, toward China, his posture militarily erect, shoulders square.

"We lost to *Gungtsetang,* the communists. To the Red political chief, Mao Tse-tung. Very smart man. He reached the peasants, and they went to him, like fish to sea. We lost to the Red generals, Chu Teh and Lin Piao, who fought like Sun-tzu, master of war.

"That's why we're here. We did not fight so well." The pain on my father's face was profound. His features did not move, but his eyes looked so vacantly sad, so ineffably alone. It was a war he needed to win and could not afford to lose.

"Your mother missed home." He coughed a little, squaring his shoulders to the window, filling his small, dark pipe with Edgeworth, a prize in wartime China. Sometimes I thought that the Nationalist Army had fought the war for Virginia tobacco. He lit the pipe, his own shadow playing on the walls, and he slipped into Songhai.

"In a way, the war goes on. The Reds might still be kicked out, and we could return to Kiangsu, where everyone but you was born. The Nationalists, my old army, are not a lot better than the Reds, but they won't kill *us.* I don't want to go back. I am American. But it might be better for you."

Better for me. Father, talking to me in our true tongue, talking about Mother. Oh, Mah-mee. I wanted him to keep talking, to never stop. Drunk on his words, intoxicated with the communication. He was talking about somehow returning to China. But I was having a hard time figuring out how to be black, how to be American. Now I had to learn to be Chinese? To go to China now, with our mother dead.

Here I had Toussaint, and Titus McGovern and Alvin Sharpes. I had Toussaint's momma, who hugged me, spoke to me with laughter in her voice, and had sung to me. A number of other women on the block were likewise kind, wiping my blood with white hankies. Hector had just saved my life, and he and Joe Cutty had great coin on the street. Reverend Jones always smiled at me, welcoming me to his church. I was not sure that I would be so lucky on the streets of Shanghai, trying to get by as a cultural Chinese. I could hardly speak Songhai anymore. The idea of backtracking on the Chinese tongues made me ill.

I, of course, in my eclectic upbringing, would have an opportunity to try that, as well.

"When you are older," he said, "I can teach you to use a gun and to knife-fight. To patrol and ambush, call in artillery fire. Military combat." He chuckled, an unusual sound. "But these are things the Army will teach you."

He shook his head. "But I am not expert at fighting with my fists." He unlocked a drawer in his desk. He pulled out a huge gun, snugged inside a light tan shoulder holster. He untied the restraining straps, the dust rising softly in the lamplight.

He looked so strong, so handsome, his jaw square, shoulders broad, the scar on his temple pronounced, his eyes far away, thinking, seeing memories, touching China and his former world.

The gun came out of the holster, complaining against the leather. It was a Government Colt Super .38 on a .45 frame. It looked heavily used, with the dark bluing worn away down to cold steel around the trigger housing and the hammer. It fit in his muscular hand like a big Thorson wrench in Hector's grip. I smelled the light oil on it. Given to him by Na-men Schwartzhedd after the Japanese invasion, it had become a talisman, an invitation to fight the enemy and survive, to find new life in the New World, to become one with the gun and with the country that had forged it from the hardest elements in the earth.

Jennifer Sung-ah had told me stories about Father during the Run. So I knew this gun had been inside his peasant jacket on the Yangtze River road, when he had found Mother and my sisters at the edge of Free China, when he had lowered his recently injured forehead to rest it against my mother's face, nine years ago.

"I know you," he had said to Mother that day in 1944. "You don't give up. You would never give up."

He snapped the action, locking it open and removing the well-worn magazine, verifying that it was empty by inserting his little finger into the breech. I was nervous, looking at it. This gun had killed people.

"When you go in the Army, this will be yours. This is not to be touched until then. I am showing this to you, because weapons are for war, for death. Never confuse this with *wu-shu.*"

I didn't know that I was going in the Army. I thought they gave you a gun, which was the only reason I could think of for joining.

He frowned at me, releasing the lock, which made the slide snap shut with a startling metallic punch. He locked the magazine into the butt of the handle, slid the weapon into the holster, and put it away.

"You have been beaten badly. Children expect parents to fix things. But you need boxing, to stand on your own.

"My older brother Han was a good boxer. The Chinese invented boxing, *wu-shu,* and are the best at it, a secret foreigners do not know. Chinese boxers are almost like magic, they are so good.

"Uncle Han's nose was broken and our mother stopped his lessons, and mine before they began. Han is a very handsome man, like a movie actor, and Mother feared for his looks. I am sorry you have never

met my brother. Uncle Han and I. We, we were not
friends. But I am his Younger Brother, and always will
be, regardless of what I do. You have not met your
grandfather, grandmother. Your aunts. The tutors. The
cooks, servants.''

"Where Han Dababa now?" I asked.

"Aahh," he sighed quietly, like dying seltzer bub-
bles. There had been no word about Uncle Han at all.
He, and Da-ma, my aunt, and Round Pearl, Mother's
servant, Wang the fish cook, Chief Tutor Luke, the
Hanlin master, Tutor Tang, and the horsemaster Yip,
and Janie's wetnurse, Sweet Plum, all were lost in the
distant haze of invasion and the Chinese revolution.
Gung-Gung, of course, had been terminally reedu-
cated. But Father missed the staff of his family more
than the management. His father had treated him like
yesterday's newspaper.

He went to the kitchen, where he blindly rattled in
the cupboards. The kitchen smelled of sauerkraut and
scrapple, a flat, cerealed, pork Pennsylvania Dutch
sausage that Edna was trying to sell to our palates.

I was intoxicated with the information he had provided me, and my bruises were forgotten. I felt shaky,
shuddering in emotion, electrified by his communication.

My father, his other life, a big gun in our house, a
boxing uncle named Han, a nation of fighting Chinese,
the Army. Was I to join his Kuomintang Army, or the
U.S. Army, which was taking so many men from the
neighborhood for Korea?

Wu-shu. Fighting talent, or fight arts, something like
that. Something deep in my shallow years, so mysterious in my utter simplicity, so ancient in my youth, con-
nected to a distant land and long-dead ancestors. Deep
racial memory. *Wu-shu* was magical fighting. Combat
by ghost warriors, faster than dreams, stronger than
concrete, war using wind, iron, and fire.

From the kitchen, where the intense bare bulb cast
light that was both too bright and insufficient, he said,

"I am going to send you to the Y, the Young Men's Christian Association. I think my wife will agree."

I coughed, and said, softly, "Ba-Ba. Stepma Edna my ma-ma? And Janie's ma-ma? *Real* ma-ma?"

Silence came from the kitchen. He approached me, looking down. I looked up. "She thinks of you as stepchildren," he said. "But you must give her the respect that you would give your mother."

"Stepma Edna want me go Y.M.C.A?" I asked.

"I think so," he said. "The Y will teach you to fight, how to protect yourself. I want you to try very hard and learn. It will probably hurt.

"It was the same for me. At St. John's College, and Taoping Academy, I was eighteen when I started learning about the ways of the West." He switched to English, clearing his throat.

"See here. America. It has the answers." His shoulders hunched and he made a huge fist, banging into the open palm of the other hand. "It has *the answers*!" His voice rang passionately through the apartment, and I knew that Edna and Janie were listening, from different levels in the house.

He looked up at me. More quietly, he said, "If you are very good—terrific, terrific, good—you can make application to West Point, someday, to make us proud. I will find Major Na-men, and ask his advice. He is West Pointer. Maybe he help get you in. It is something, the only thing, I pray for."

Father *praying*? Praying for me to be an American *ping*—a soldier. A small, white ivory figure on a dark teak Chinese chessboard. My heart pounded.

"Where Major Na-men, Father?" I asked.

"He is in Korea. Ahh. How I worry about him." Father's face said everything, with all the articulation Mother had used. And I knew, with sweeping, insightful clarity, that Father would have been long in Korea, with his true comrade, fighting the Reds, laughing at death, if he had not had children. Or a dying wife. Or a new one. That his family was a barrier to a greater destiny. He was passing time with us, while greater events marched past his window.

More solemn shadows flared as he lit his pipe, the sound of the drawing air strained and high.

Our magical talk was over. I found myself crying helplessly. This was so hard, crying in front of him, but his words, his sharing, his interest, the weight of his own loss caused by me, were more than I could bear. My shoulders shaking, my arms trembling uselessly by my side, I snorted and snuffled as I tried to stop myself.

My crying discomforted him. I sensed that he wanted me to shake his hand and say thank you in a manful way, and not turn into a quivering, protoplasmic blubber of tears.

I thought of my mother. He had said "us." I stood and left the room, going to the place in the hallway where her portrait had hung until Edna had removed it. I closed my wet eyes and mentally drew in every detail of her face and smiled when I reached her mouth.

11

BANQUET

My father was feeling no guilt, when there were those who felt he should. He had enjoyed a certain beau-geste reputation in Chinatown, a condition only enhanced by his tragic widowerhood. But he married a *nahgwangning* widow with flaming blond hair and a chest designed to make the majority of Chinese women on Grant Avenue look at their mirrors twice.

The new bride wrinkled her nose at the best Chinese banquet dishes outside the Far East, made no effort to learn the Chinese language or customs, and kept expanding her chest at people when she felt threatened.

The Ting Hui, our Family Association, was notable for its broad spectrum of personalities, its unique domination by Northern Chinese, and its consistent ability to mistakenly order unbalanced banquet dishes. For reasons unknown, there had been no Ting Hui in north China, while there was one in the south. Our Association had no deep tradition of ordering routinely for seventy people.

Banquets should involve correct ratios of fish, fowl, beef, and pork, vegetables and soup, tea and rice wine. But our Hui, or *tong*, often spoke Cantonese with the

clarity of Sippy Suds reciting *Hamlet*. A misplaced
tone, an awkward emphasis, and chicken wings appeared in lieu of Peking duck. When the unparalleled
elegance of birds'-nest and sharks'-fin soups was appropriate, we got egg drop broth. If the final fish dish
were supposed to be ling cod, we had rock. Squab was
ordered but extra portions of abalone wrapped in Tien-
tsin cabbage appeared.

As an American variant to Chinese food service,
each table sported a bottle of Johnnie Walker Red, a
bottle of Johnnie Walker Black, and a bottle of crème
de menthe. Our Association almost never broke the
seals and rotated turns for taking the liquor home.
Later, these bottles would be circulated as constantly
unopened, repassed, reused, and recycled gifts for
weddings, the New Year, graduations, births, or ching
ming. The trick was acquiring matching gift boxes
from liquor stores and making a five-year-old circulat-
ing bottle of alcohol appear as a new purchase. Of
course, no one was fooled, but the effort was considered essential.

"Ohh, Auntie! This looks *new*!" cried one innocent.

"Elaine! Of course it's new! It's never been
opened!"

When Father brought Edna to the Family Association Banquet celebrating the Double Ten, the new bride
was received like royalty. October 10, or Ten-Ten, is
the anniversary of the formation of the Chinese Re-
public in 1912 under Sun Yat-sen, a man admired by
both Nationalists and communists, by Chinese citi-
zens, and by the overseas communities. Jennifer Sung-
ah and Megan Wai-la also appeared, to honor Father,
to respect his new marriage, and to have a great meal.

Edna wore a deep celestial-blue, Chinese cheongsam, a side-cut mandarin-collared dress of the same
style affected by my mother when she shopped for
Cream of Wheat at Old Petrini's. This was the uniform
of the Chinatown banquet circuit after the war, before

many of the women decided to liberate themselves from dresses that made breathing a struggle. The blue set off Edna's shining blondness, and she seemed to have arrived with all the fanfare of a UCLA cheerleader, complete with tinseled searchlights, a roll of drums, and a blare of trumpets. The gallant iconoclastic killing machine, Colonel Ting, had married Marilyn Monroe and had brought her to dinner.

My sisters looked grand, and I marveled at their beauty in their similar dresses. Jennifer wore teal, Megan was in red, and Jane, because her older sisters knew she would arrive in rags, had brought her a classy, elegant black cheongsam. Our family must have looked like something out of Hollywood. Or Shanghai. The young men in the *tong* flocked around my *chiehchieh*, calling them *hsiaochieh,* or honorably desirable high-ranking unmarried misses, and I was delighted for Janie. She was having a Cinderella-like evening. Hearing her hesitant giggle, and then her fulsome laughter, made me smile with wet eyes.

I had been to banquets before and had been allowed to run around the tables with other children. I knew a few of the boys my age by name, and had missed seeing them. Edna's rule was to remain seated, and I did not know if I could move. That's not true, I corrected myself: if in doubt, don't. I strained my ears to listen to my sisters, and with a sinking sensation realized that their Songhai was too fast for me. I was losing my language. But I enjoyed looking at them whenever they passed near, and both Jennifer and Megan took time to sit next to me and tell me how handsome I looked. Janie had already explained to them why my face looked like Route 66 after a bad rain.

Leo Soo, one of the brightest kids in Chinatown, dropped by the table and sat next to me. I poured him a short cup of tea, and as he filled the balance of the cup with sugar, he asked me how our family was surviving the loss of our mother.

I smiled, putting on a brave face.

"I'm sorry, Kai," he said. "Very sorry. Mah-mee invited you and Ming-li over to spend weekends with us. But your new mother said you were too sad to leave the house."

Chinatown banquets, like West Point meals, seat ten souls in family-style tables. So I sat, poured huge mountains of sugar into my tea cup, and drank away. The food arrived, the families took their seats, our table drew all the stares, and Father explained the dishes.

"This," he said, pointing, "is called 'sea cucumbers.' But they are not vej-ah-taybles. They are ocean slugs. Yes, yes. It's terrible. See there. Chicken heads. Not cut off, since that's bad luck. So stupid! These superstitions! Cutting off heads mean, not giving *everything* to the guests. Like, holding back something valuable. So we have the head, looking back at us. Make no sense! Not cutting off fish head okay, since cheek is special. There. There is Peking duck. This is plum sauce, for the crispy skin . . . and the small bun . . . see, it breaks like this. First sauce on, then skin. . . . No, no. No waiters for this table! We serve ourselves! We're American!" He waved them away.

Jennifer helped Father serve the dishes, first for Edna, then for Megan, Janie, me, and then themselves.

"We serve the tea in the opposite order of the west," said Megan, pouring. "The first-poured tea goes to the youngest; the last-poured tea, which is the richest, the fullest, the best-steeped, goes to the eldest, or highest-ranking family member. Tonight, Edna, that is you. So I serve Kai first, then Janie."

At the earliest opportunity—after seven courses had been served—several women of the Association broke ranks and approached the elegant couple, offering greetings while frankly assessing the bride's goods.

Edna did not care about the food; she worried about the approaching women. She was extremely suspicious, but gracious, delighted to find so many bright